PETAL AND POPPY AND THE SPOOKY HALLOWEEN!

BY **LISA CLOUGH**
AND
ED BRIANT

Green Light Readers
HOUGHTON MIFFLIN HARCOURT
Boston New York

www.hmhco.com

The text of this book is set in Cheltenham.
The display type was hand-lettered.
The illustrations were created digitally.

The Library of Congress Cataloging-in-Publication Data is on file.

ISBN: 978-0-544-33603-2 paperback
ISBN: 978-0-544-33602-5 paper over board

Manufactured in China
SCP 10 9 8 7 6 5 4 3 2

4500506087

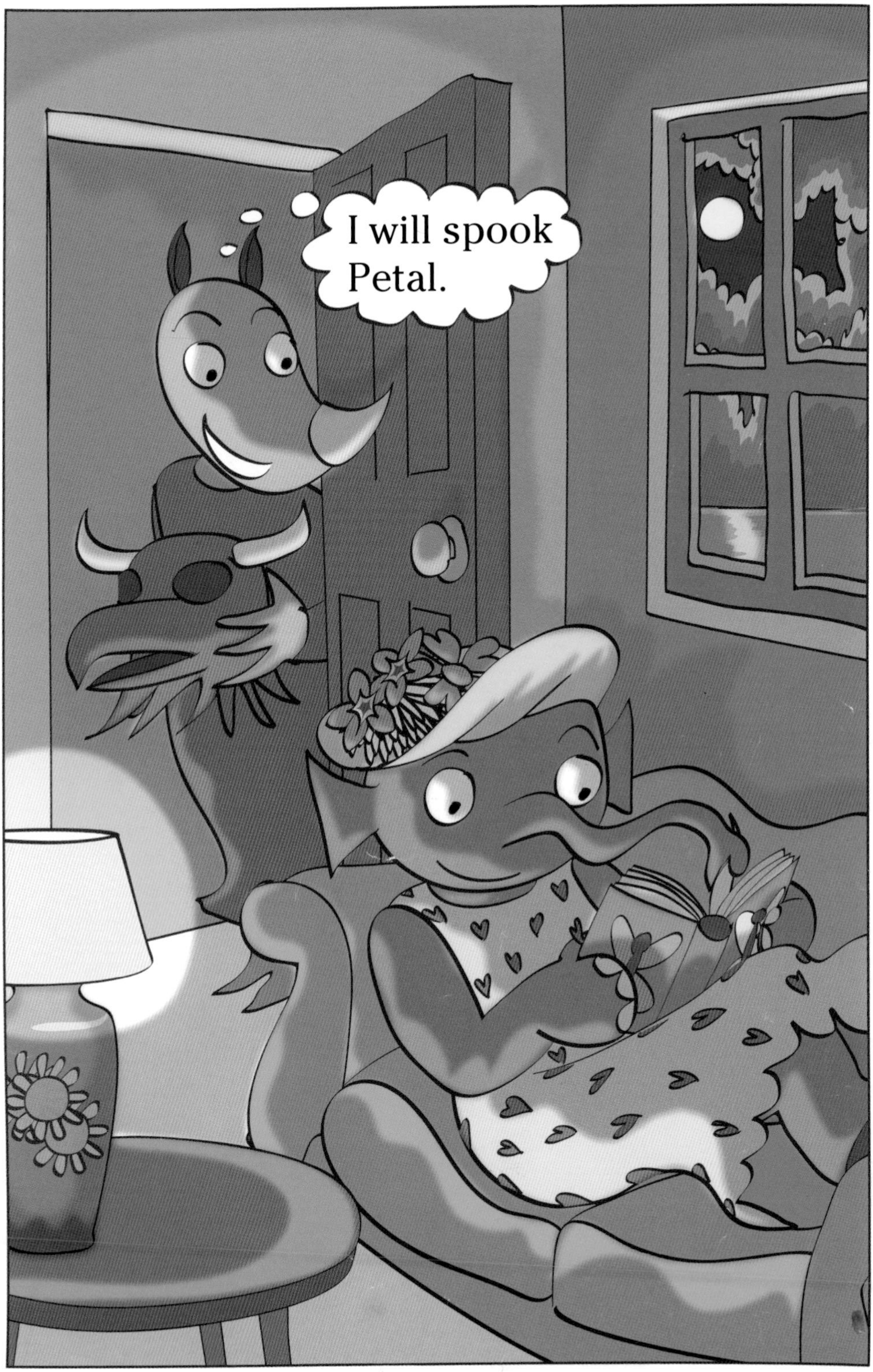
I will spook
Petal.

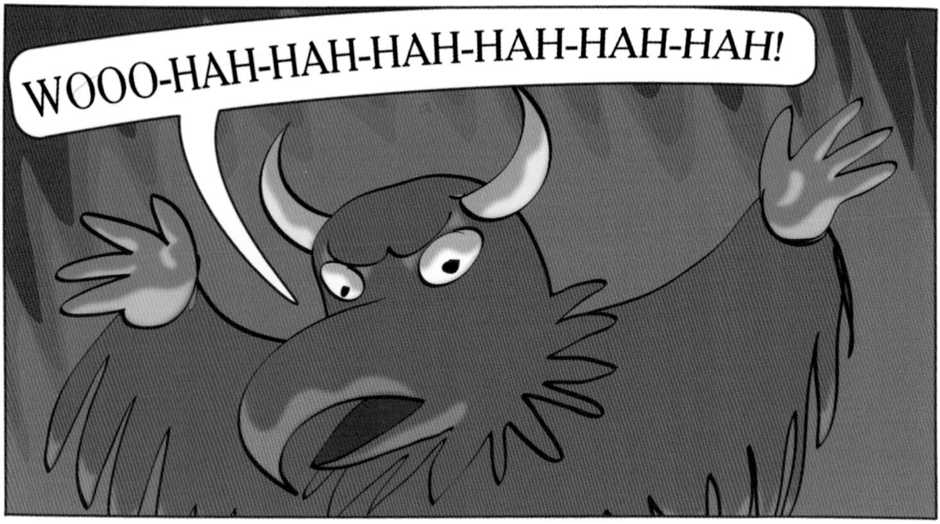
WOOO-HAH-HAH-HAH-HAH-HAH-HAH!

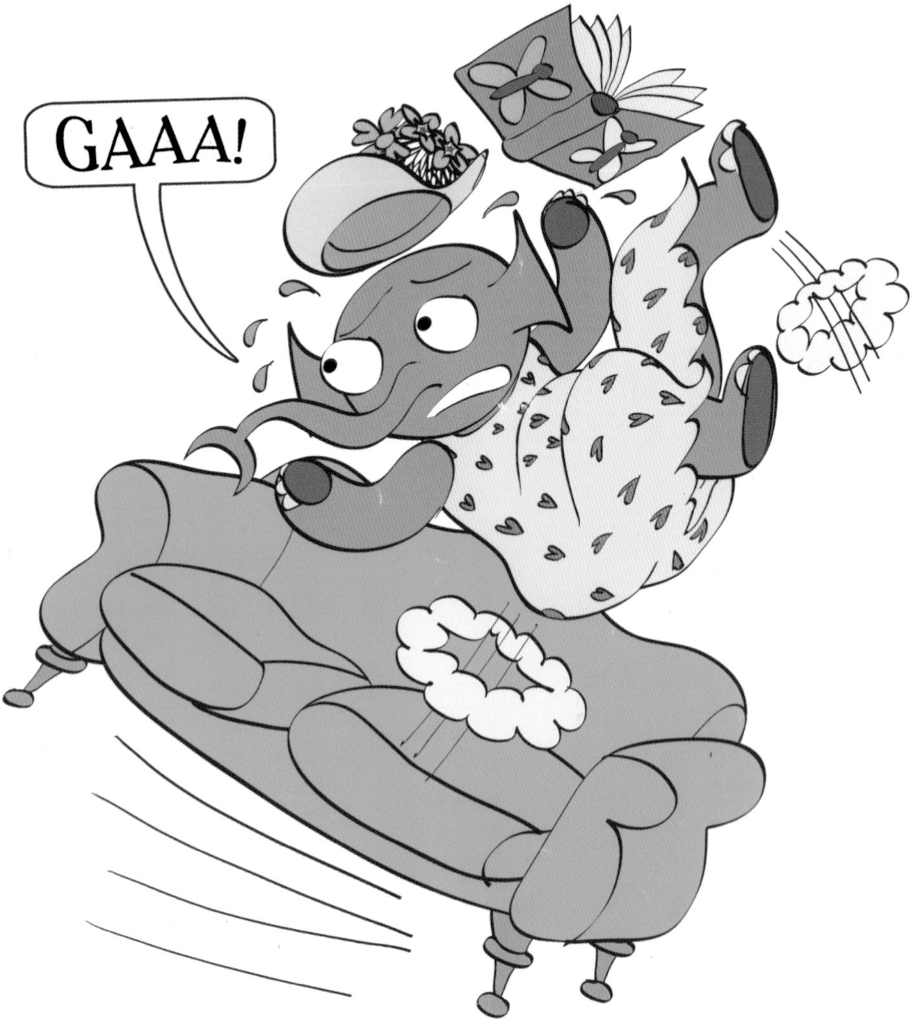
GAAA!

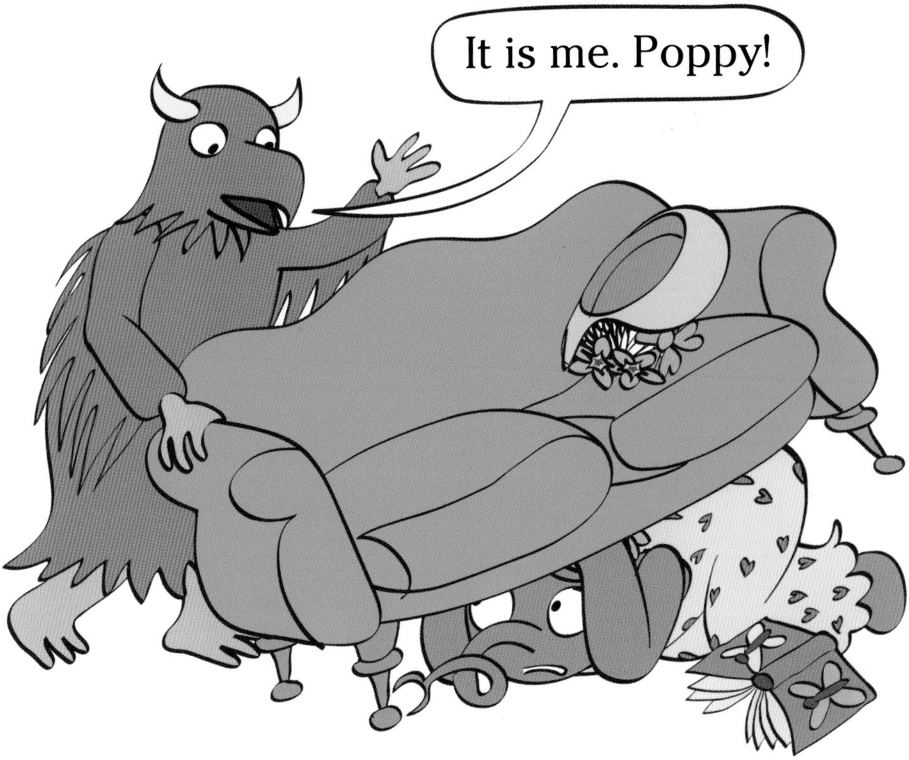
It is me. Poppy!

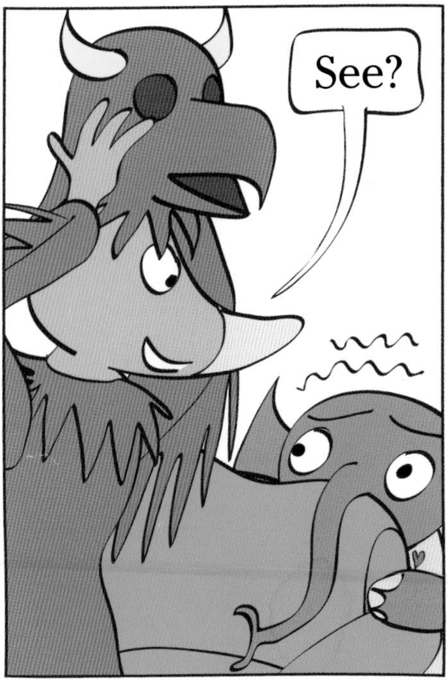
See?

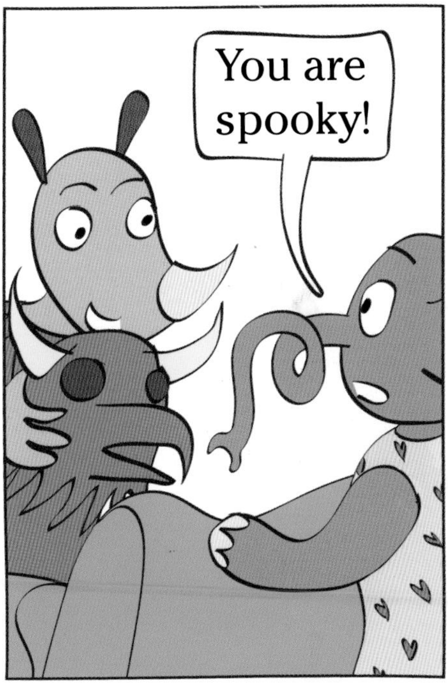
You are
spooky!

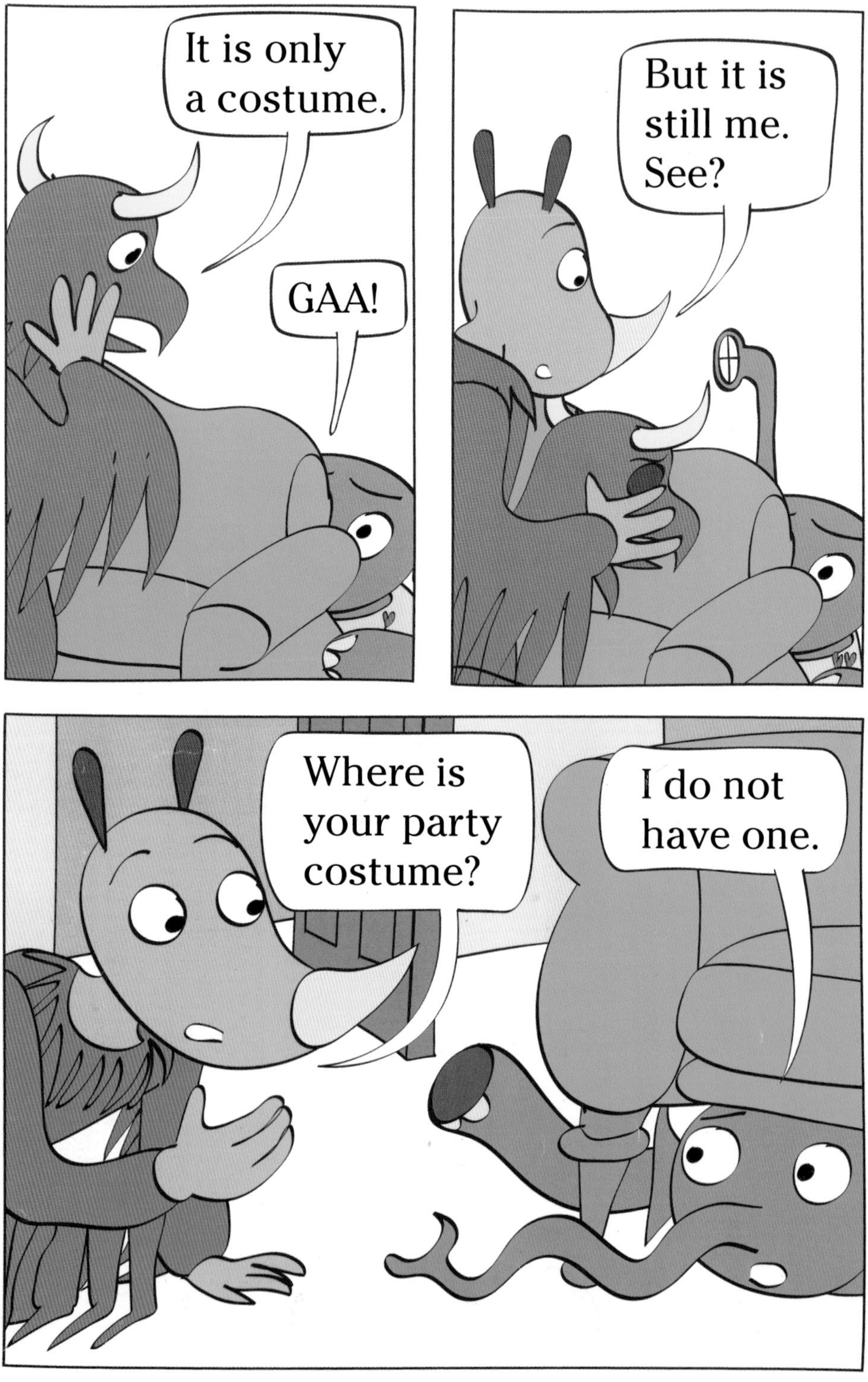
It is only a costume.
GAA!
But it is still me. See?
Where is your party costume?
I do not have one.

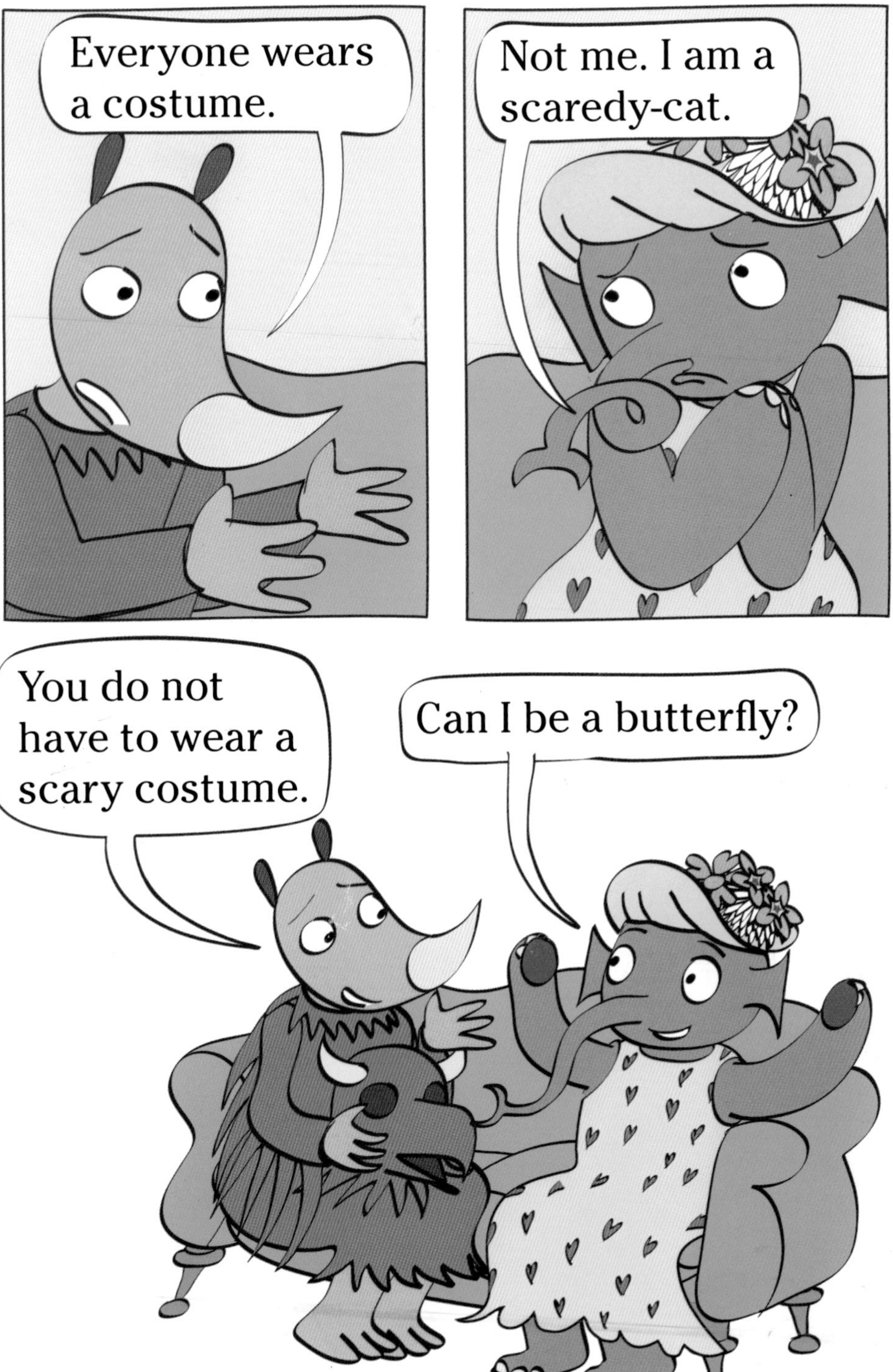
Everyone wears a costume.
Not me. I am a scaredy-cat.
You do not have to wear a scary costume.
Can I be a butterfly?

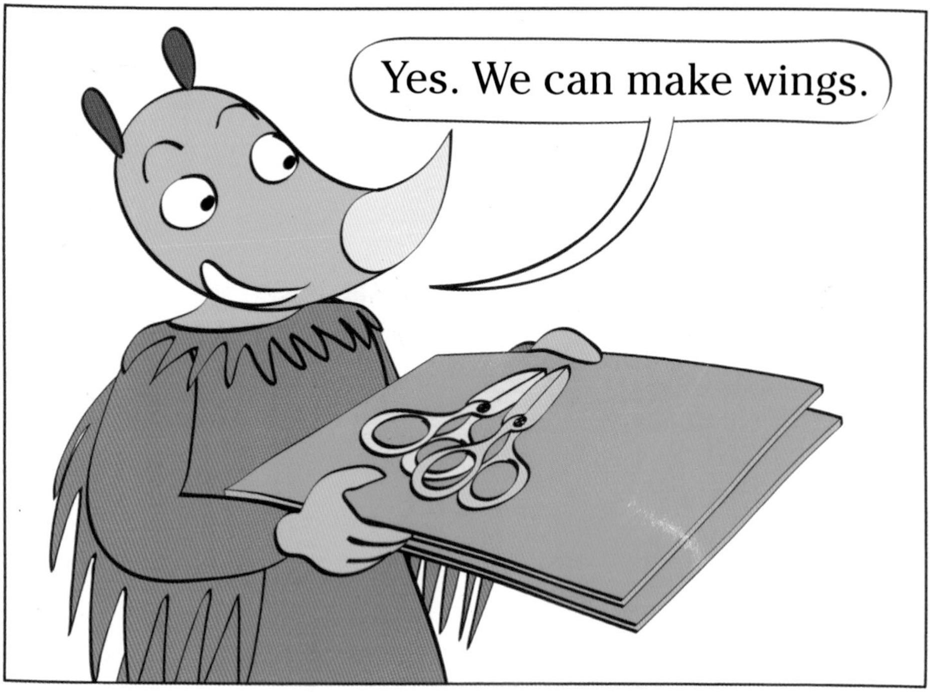
Yes. We can make wings.

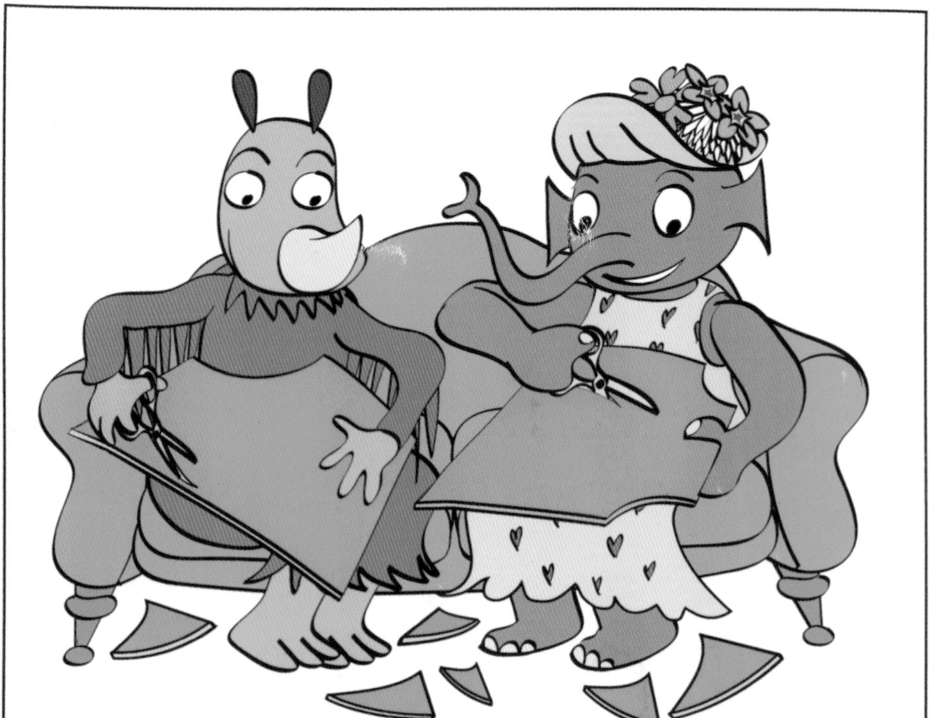

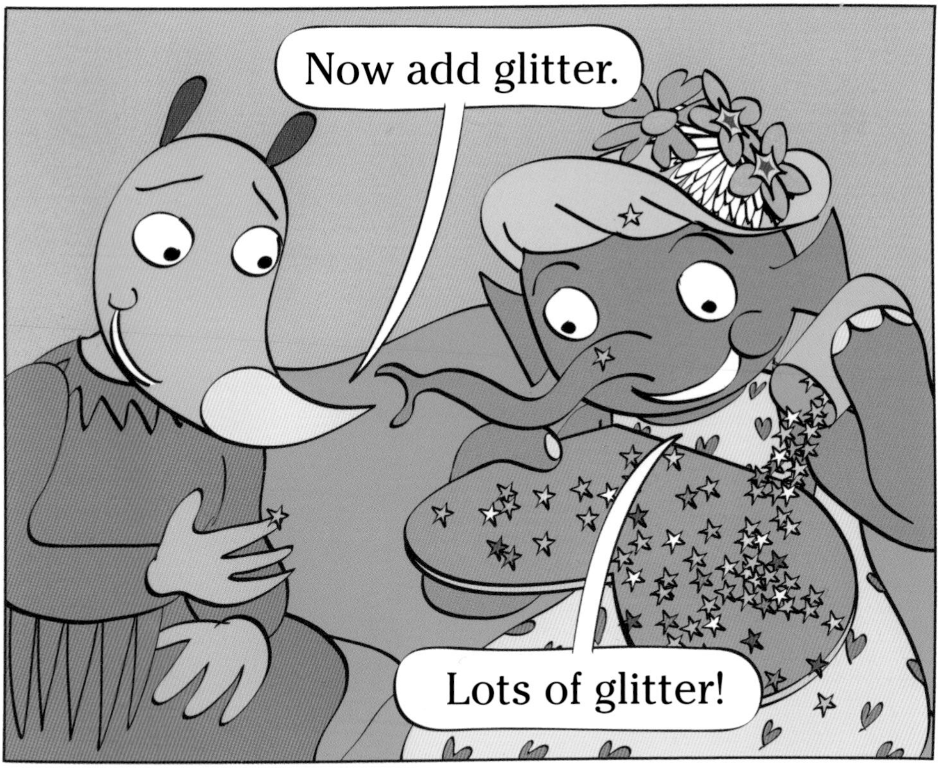
Now add glitter.
Lots of glitter!

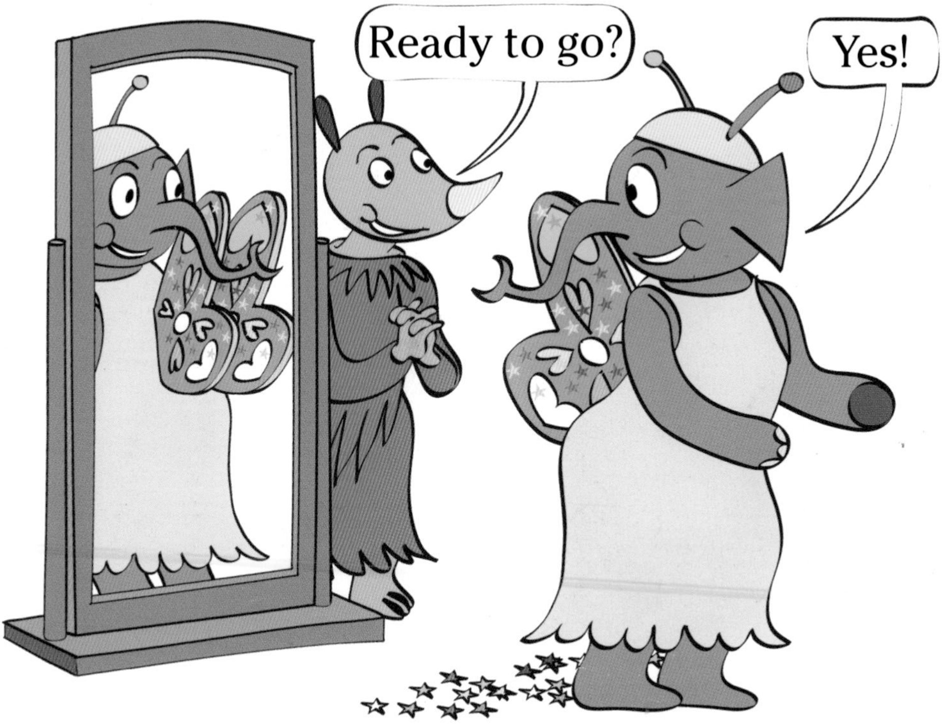
Ready to go?
Yes!

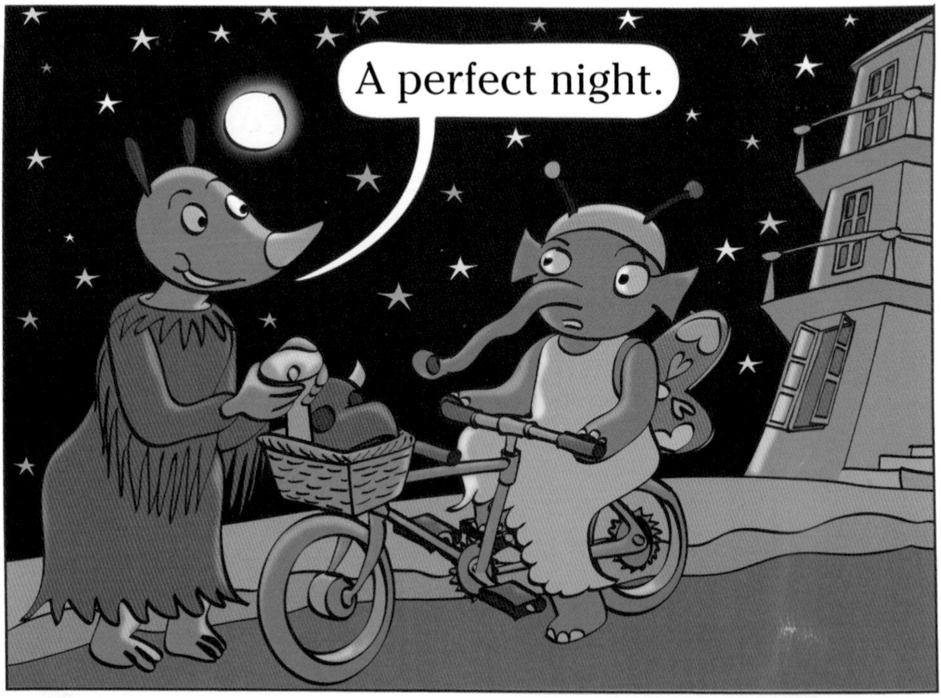
A perfect night.

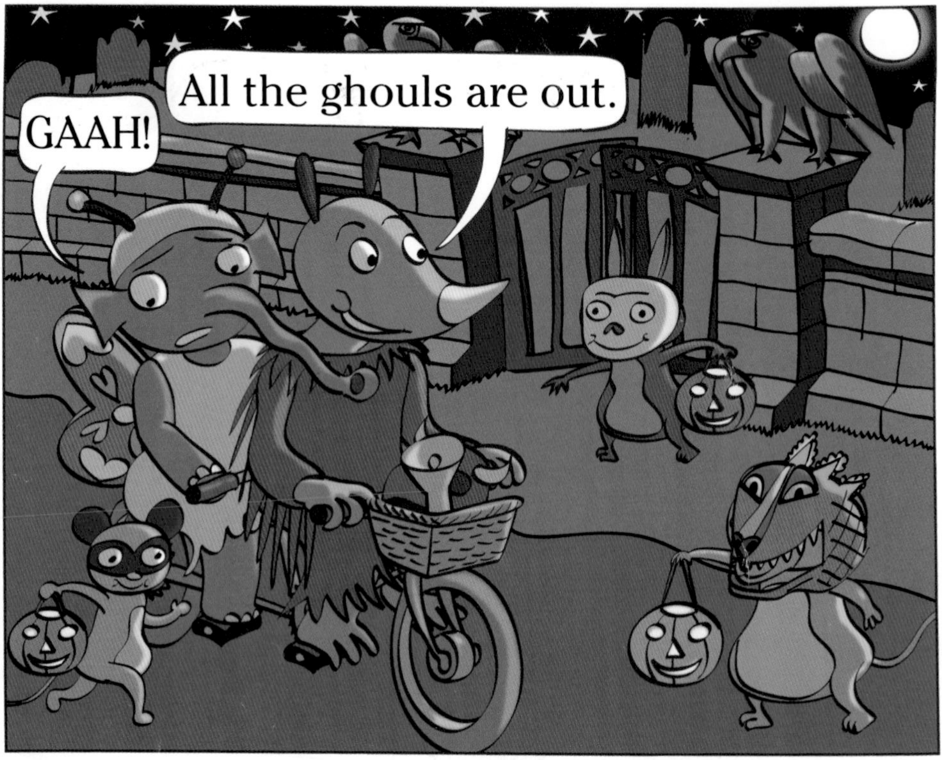
GAAH!
All the ghouls are out.

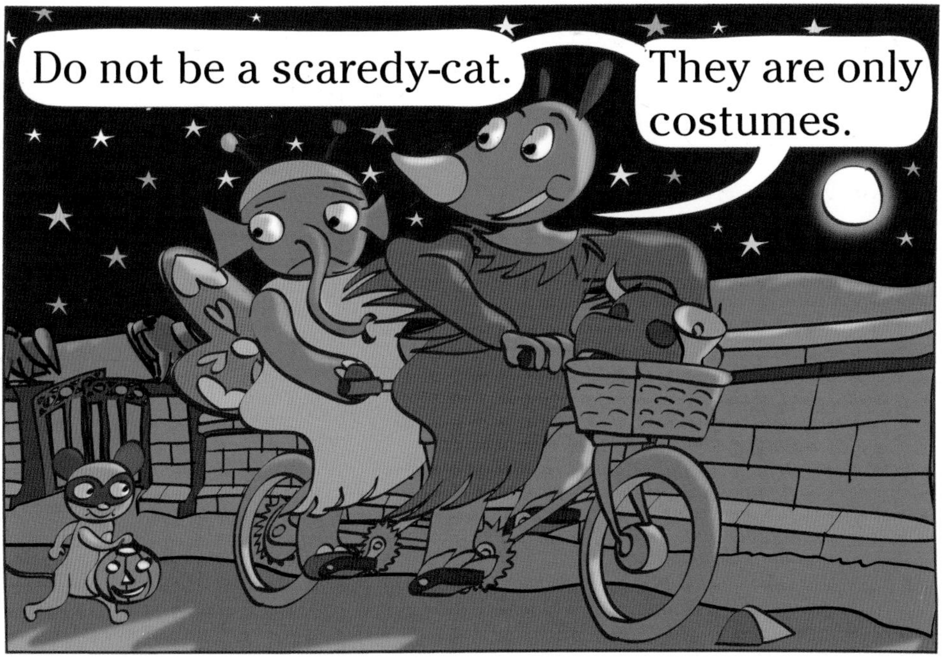
Do not be a scaredy-cat.
They are only costumes.

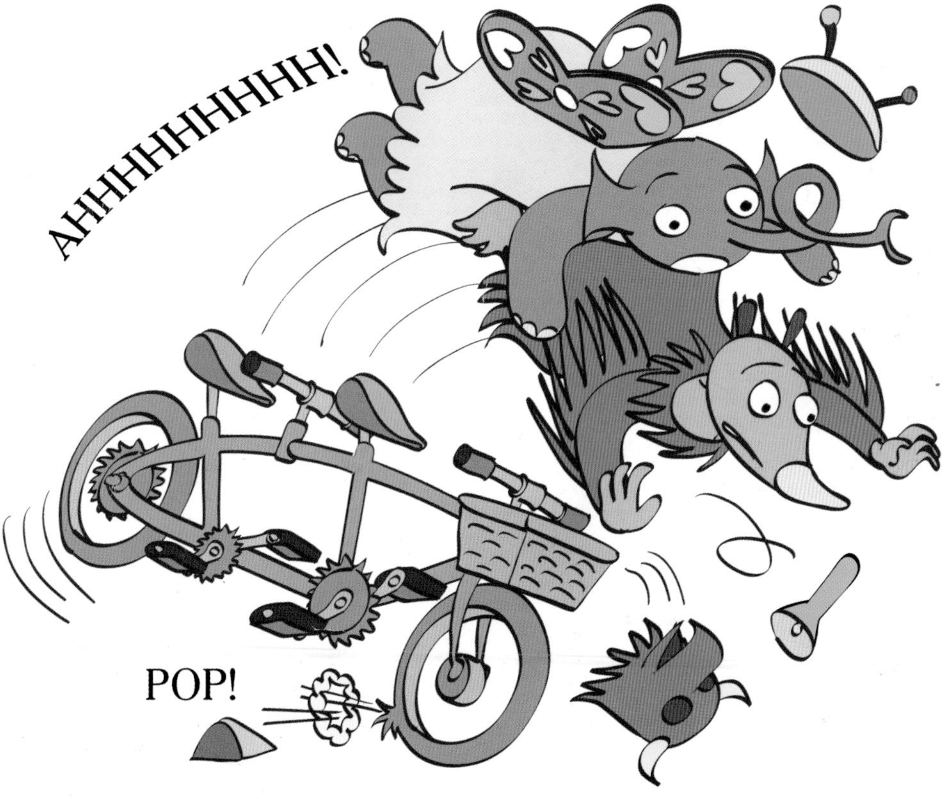
AHHHHHHHHH!
POP!

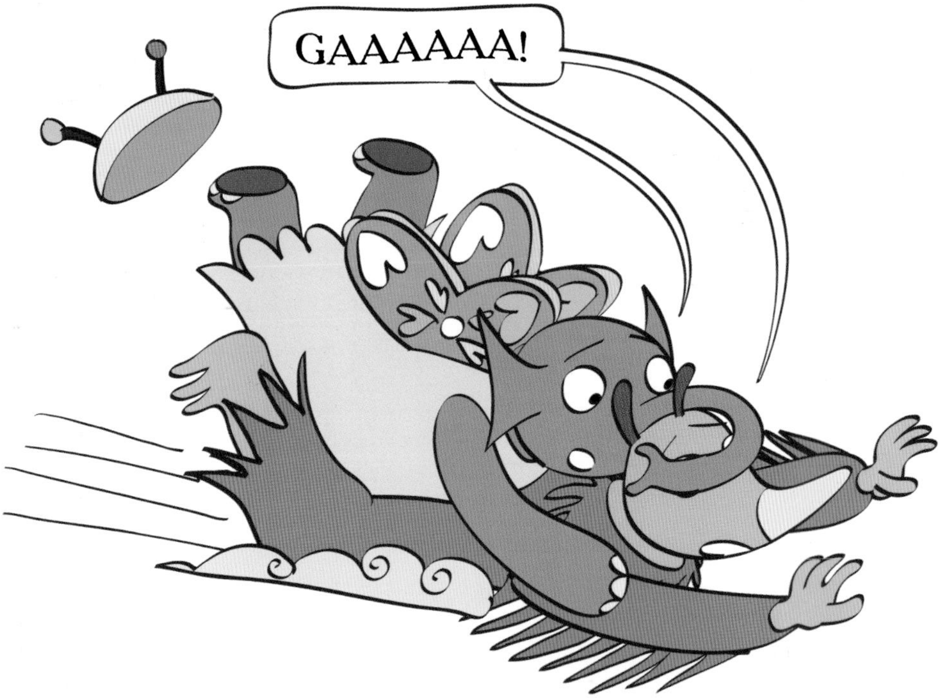
GAAAAAA!

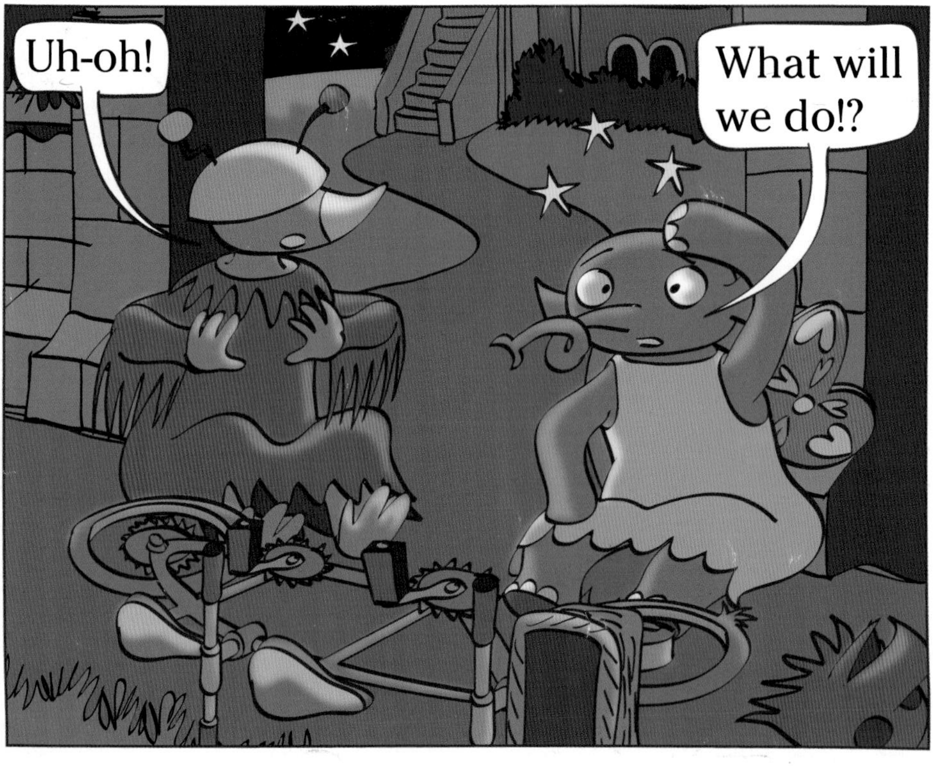
Uh-oh!
What will we do!?

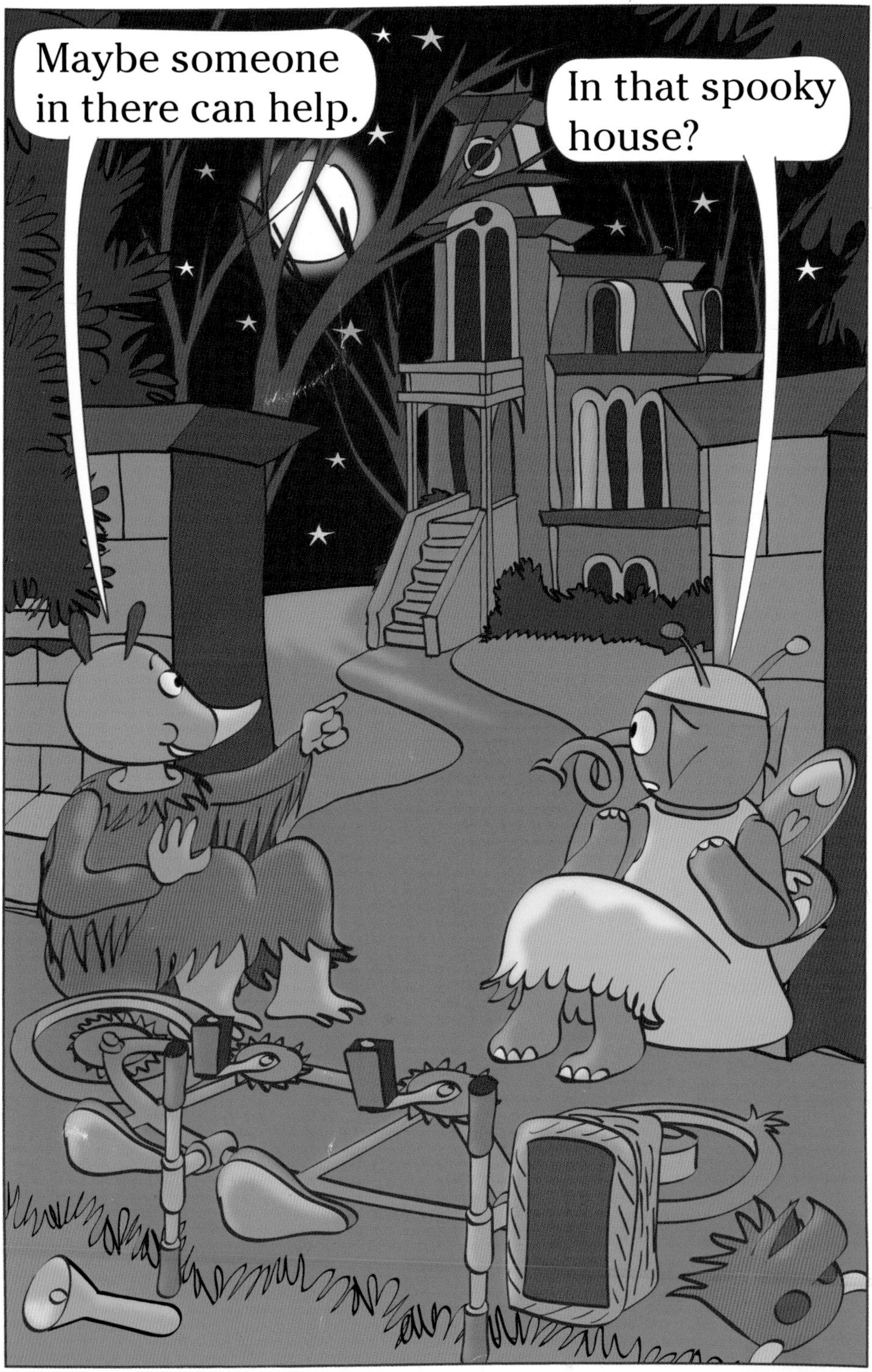
Maybe someone in there can help.
In that spooky house?

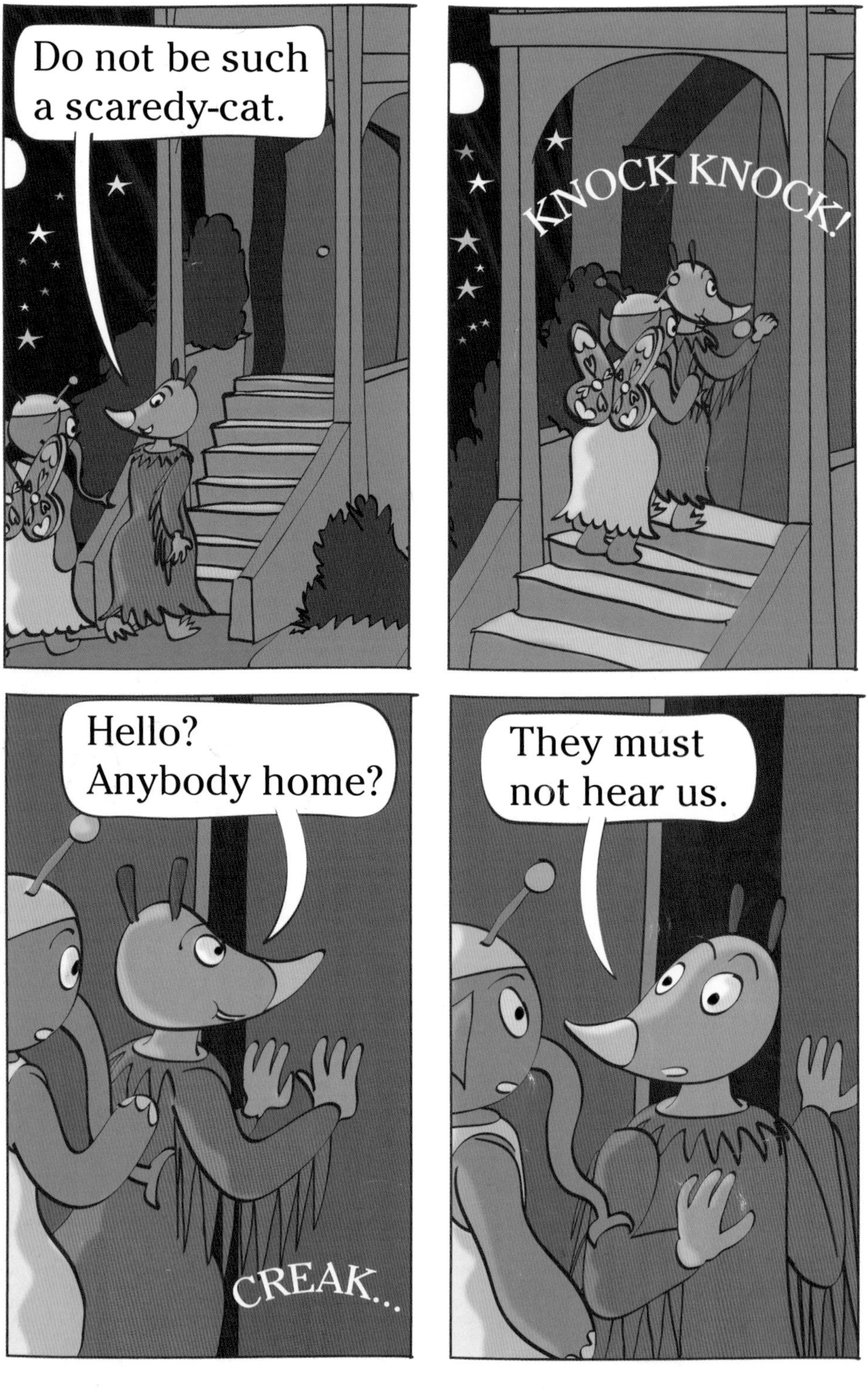
Do not be such a scaredy-cat.
KNOCK KNOCK!
Hello? Anybody home?
CREAK...
They must not hear us.

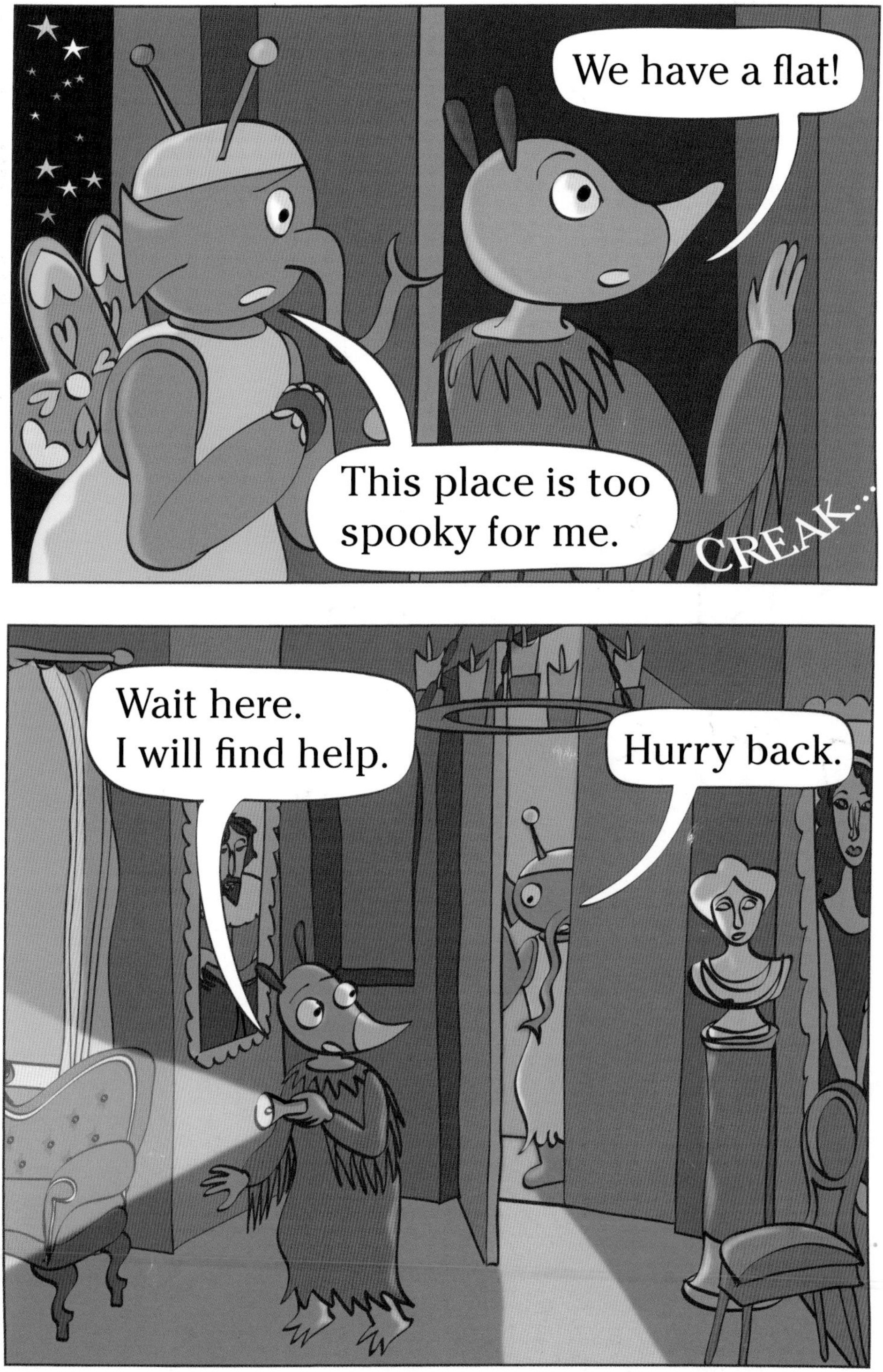
We have a flat!
This place is too spooky for me.
CREAK...
Wait here. I will find help.
Hurry back.

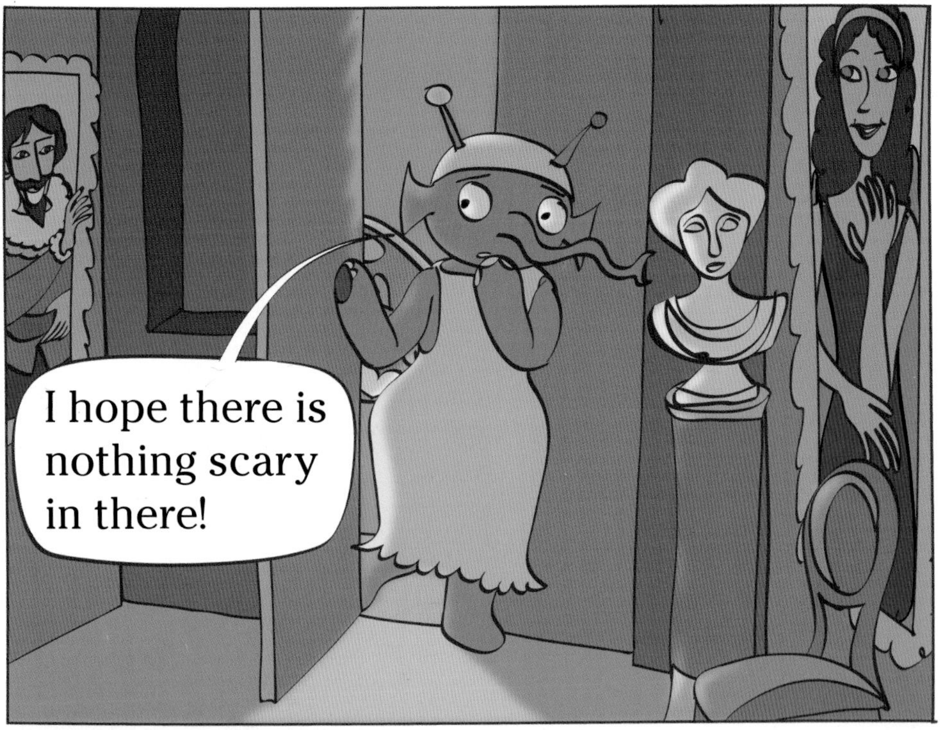
I hope there is nothing scary in there!

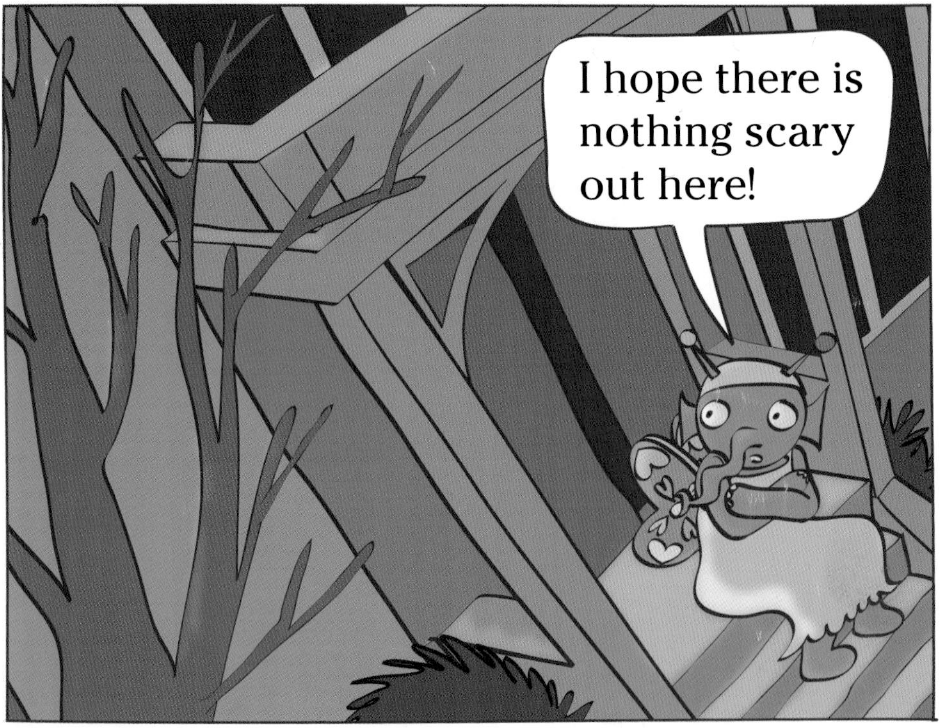
I hope there is nothing scary out here!

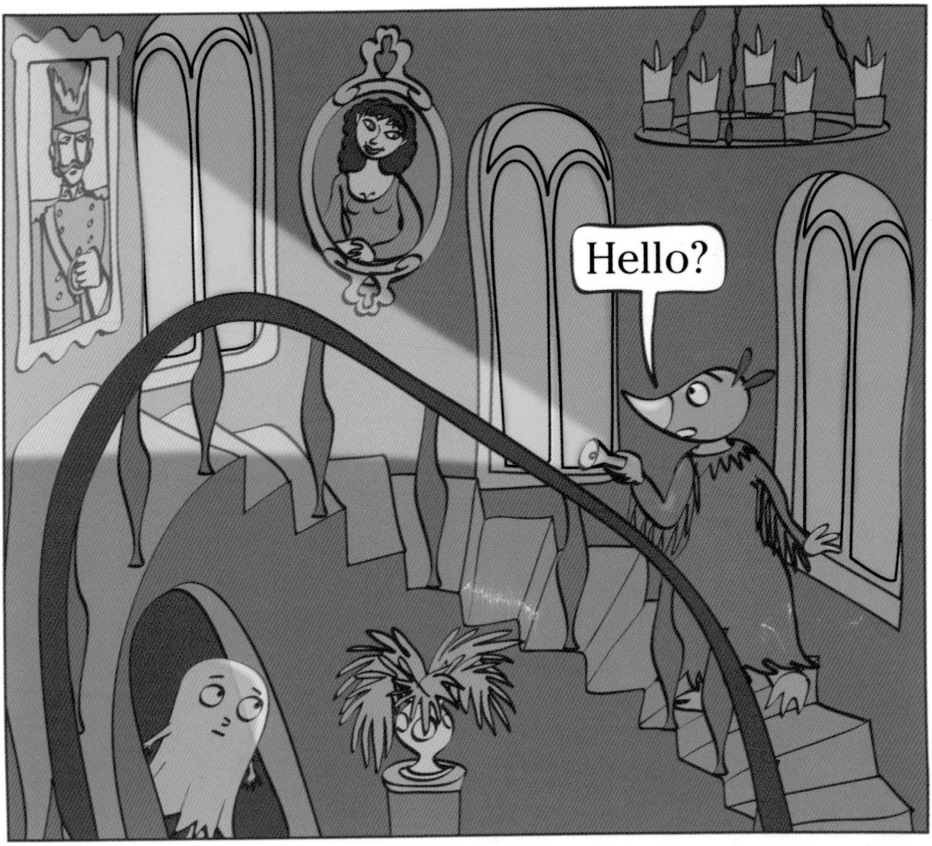
Hello?

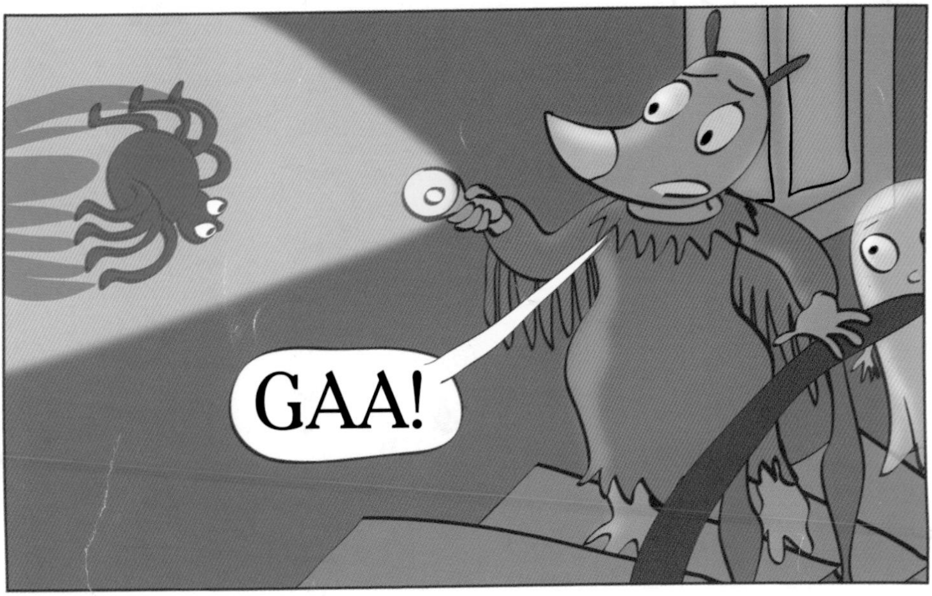
GAA!

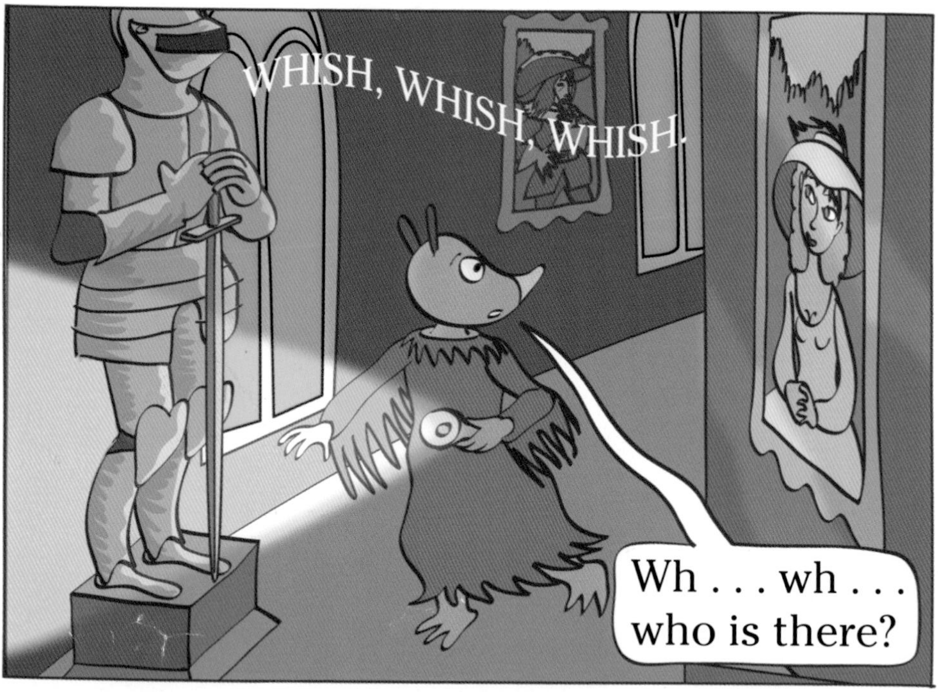
WHISH, WHISH, WHISH.
Wh . . . wh . . .
who is there?

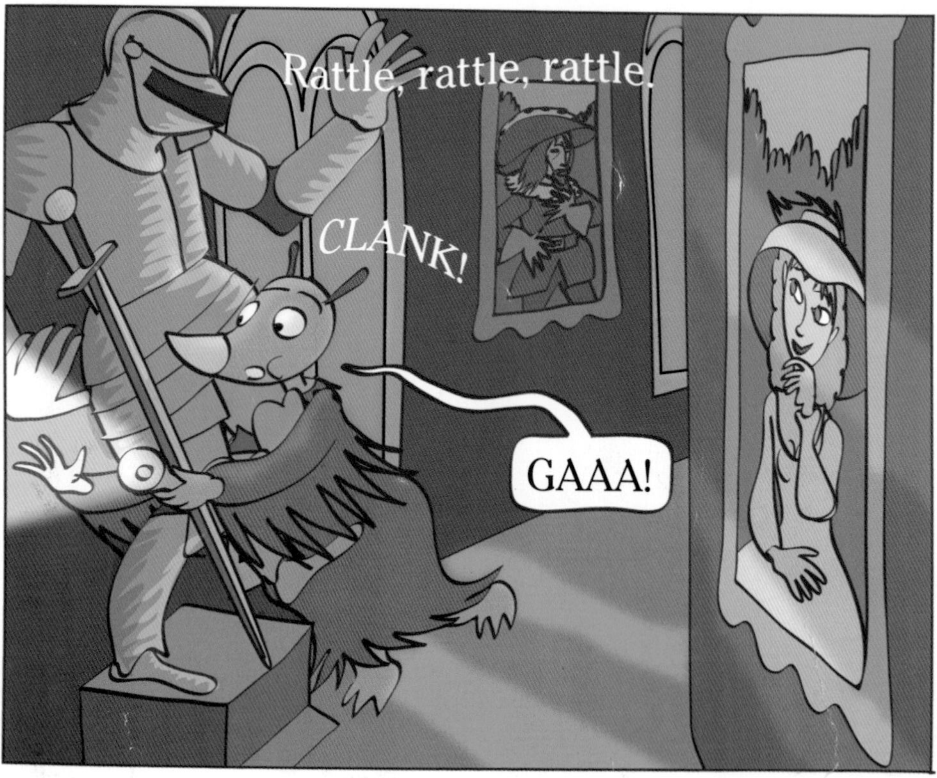
Rattle, rattle, rattle.
CLANK!
GAAA!

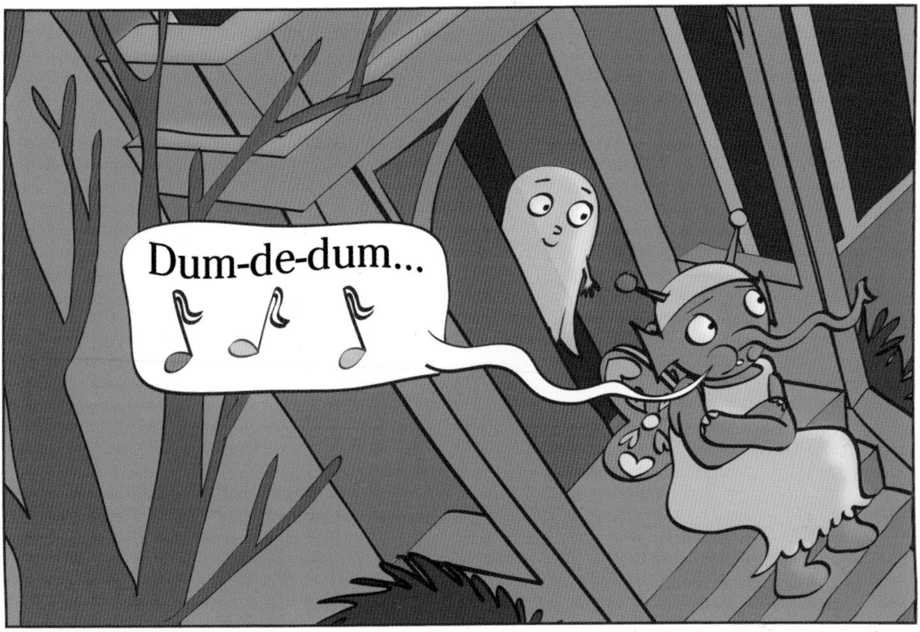
Dum-de-dum...

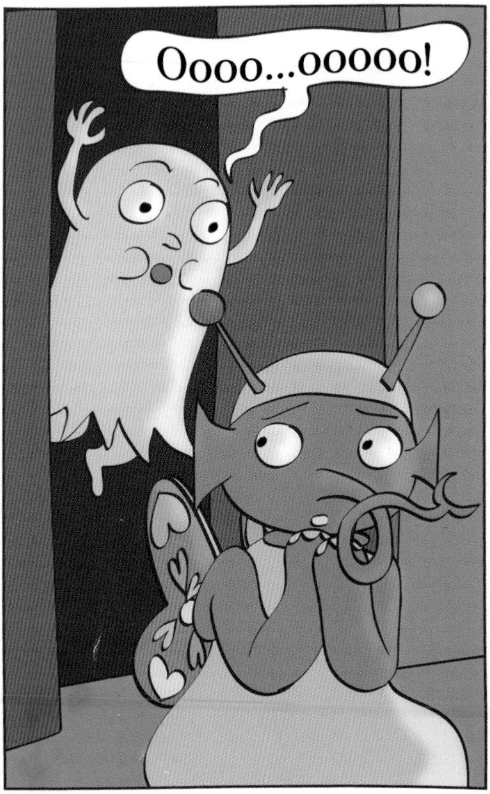
Oooo...ooooo!

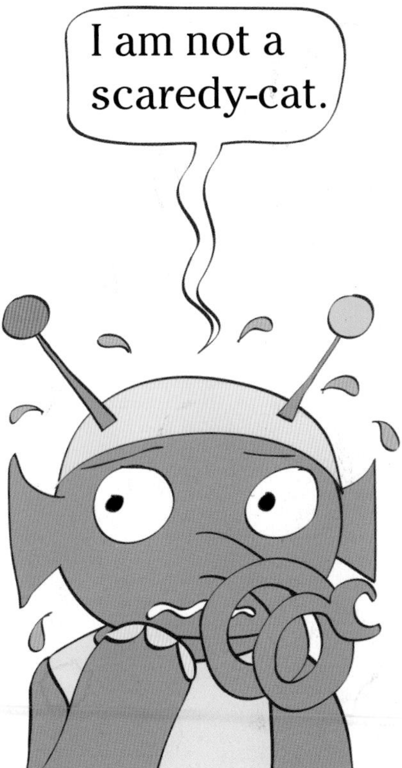
I am not a scaredy-cat.

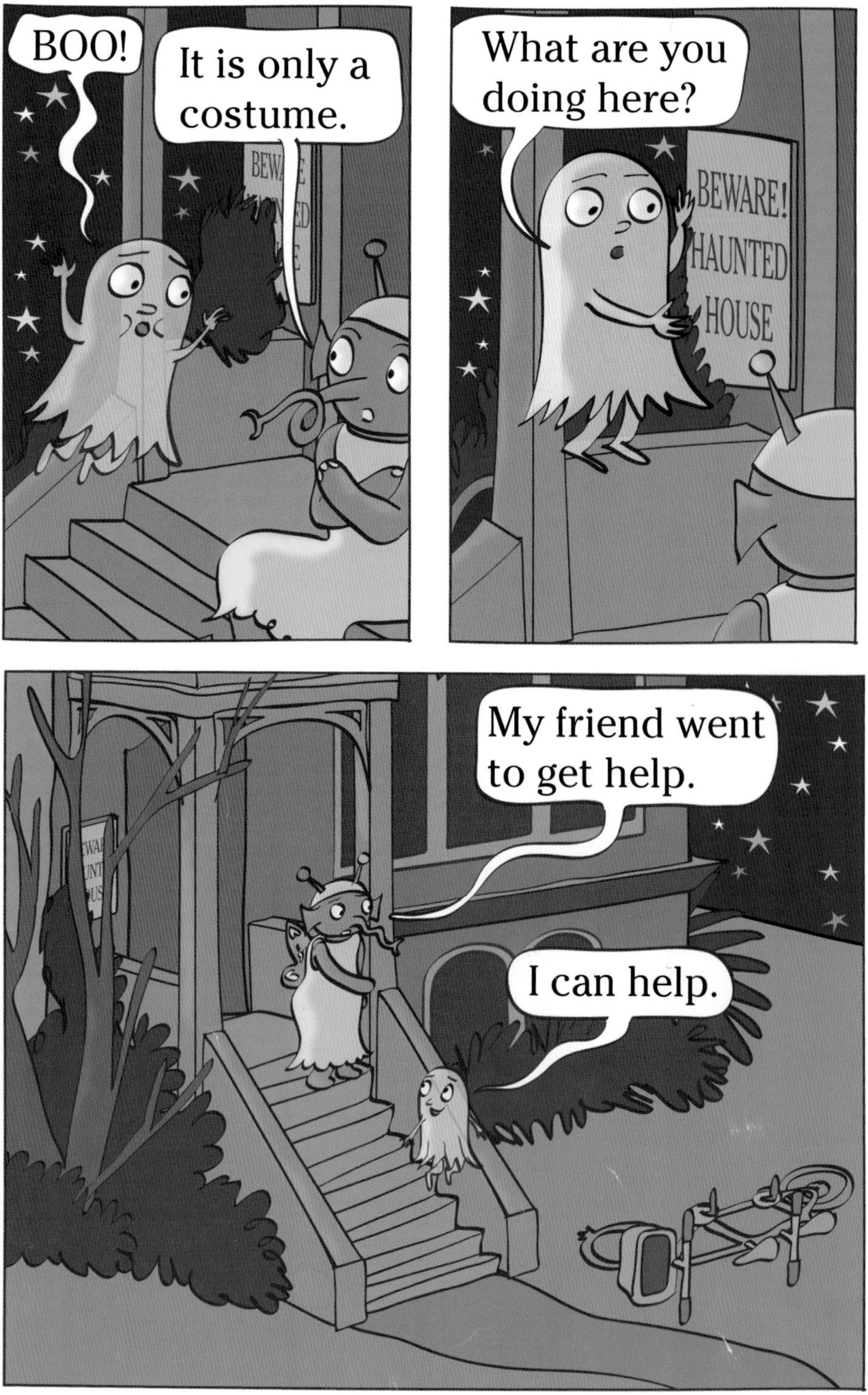
BOO!
It is only a costume.
What are you doing here?
BEWARE! HAUNTED HOUSE
My friend went to get help.
I can help.

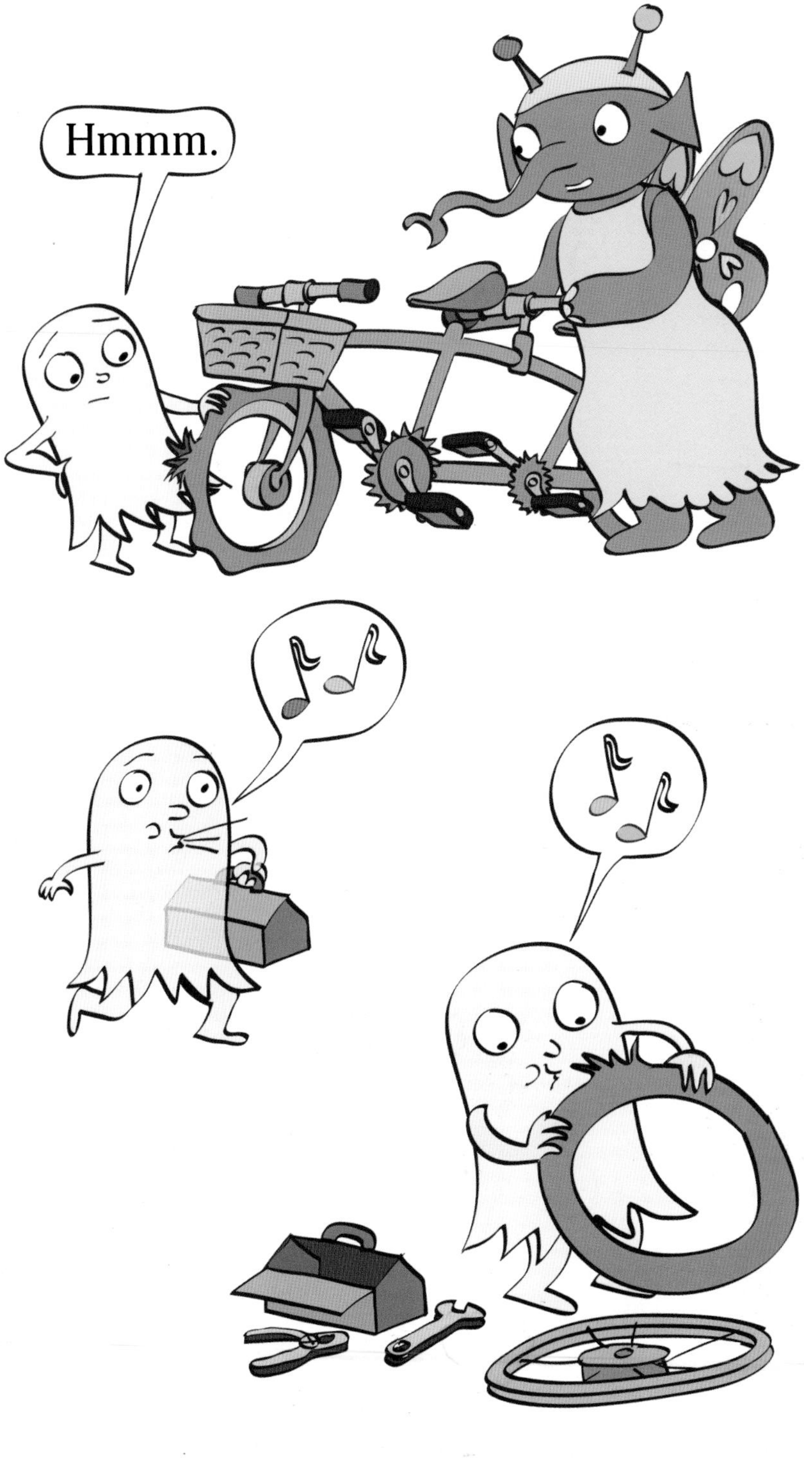
Hmmm.

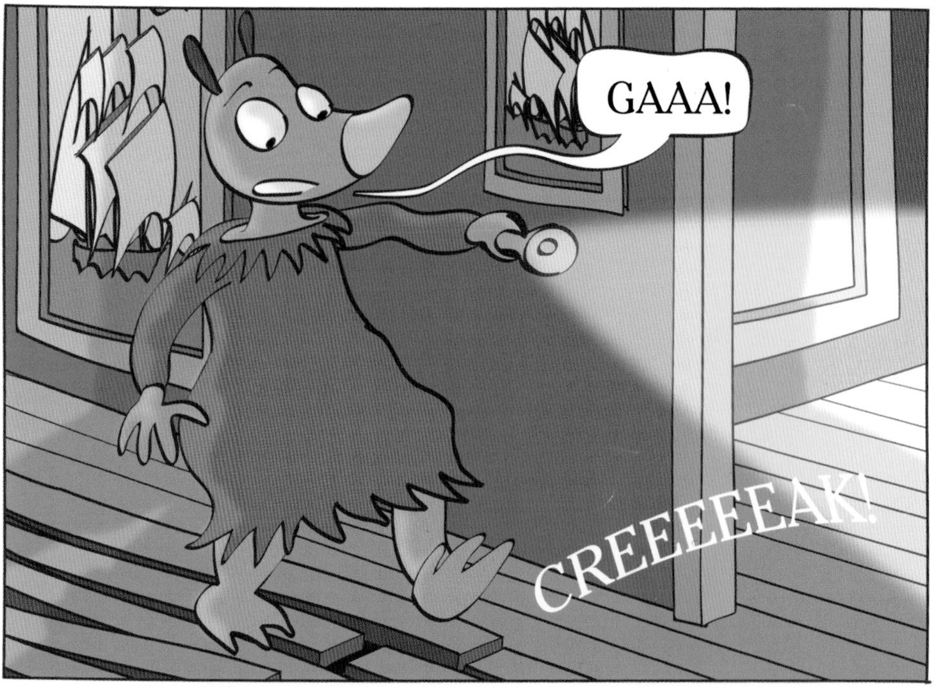
GAAA!
CREEEEEEAK!

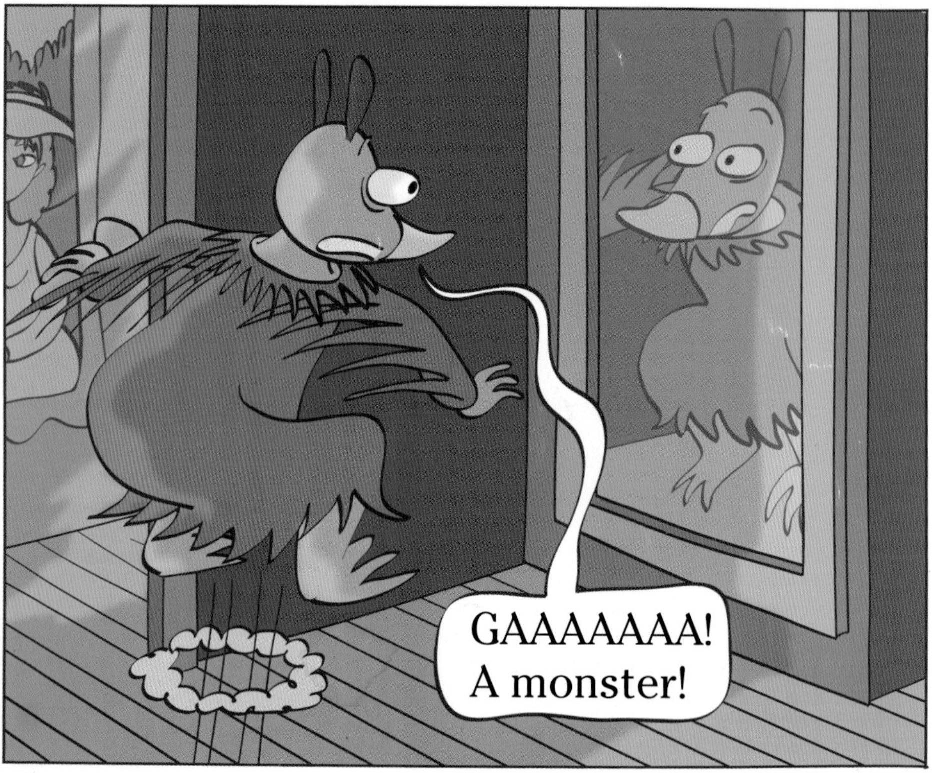
GAAAAAAA!
A monster!

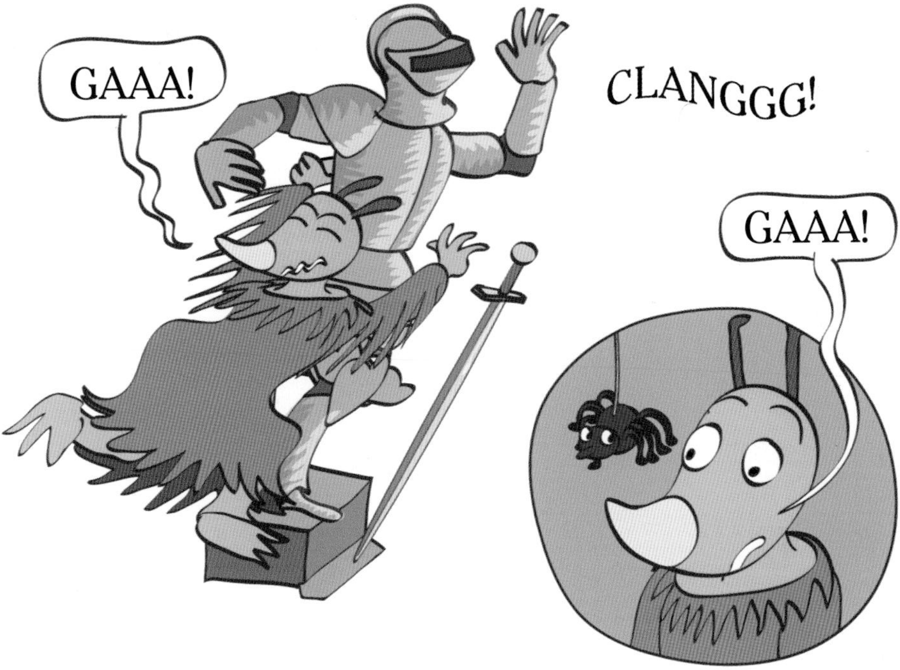
GAAA!
CLANGGG!
GAAA!

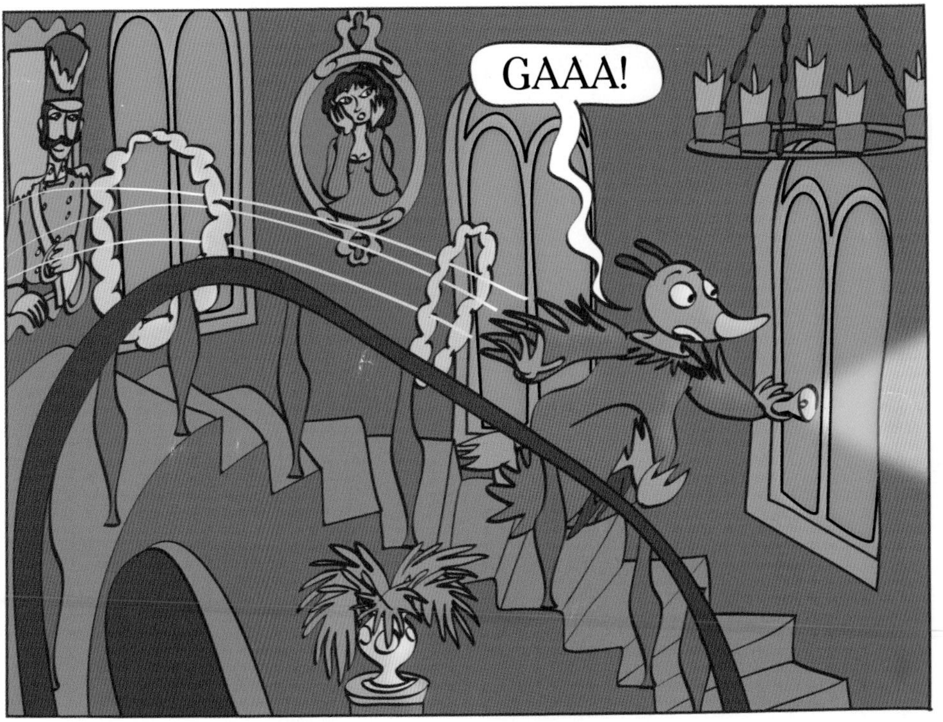
GAAA!

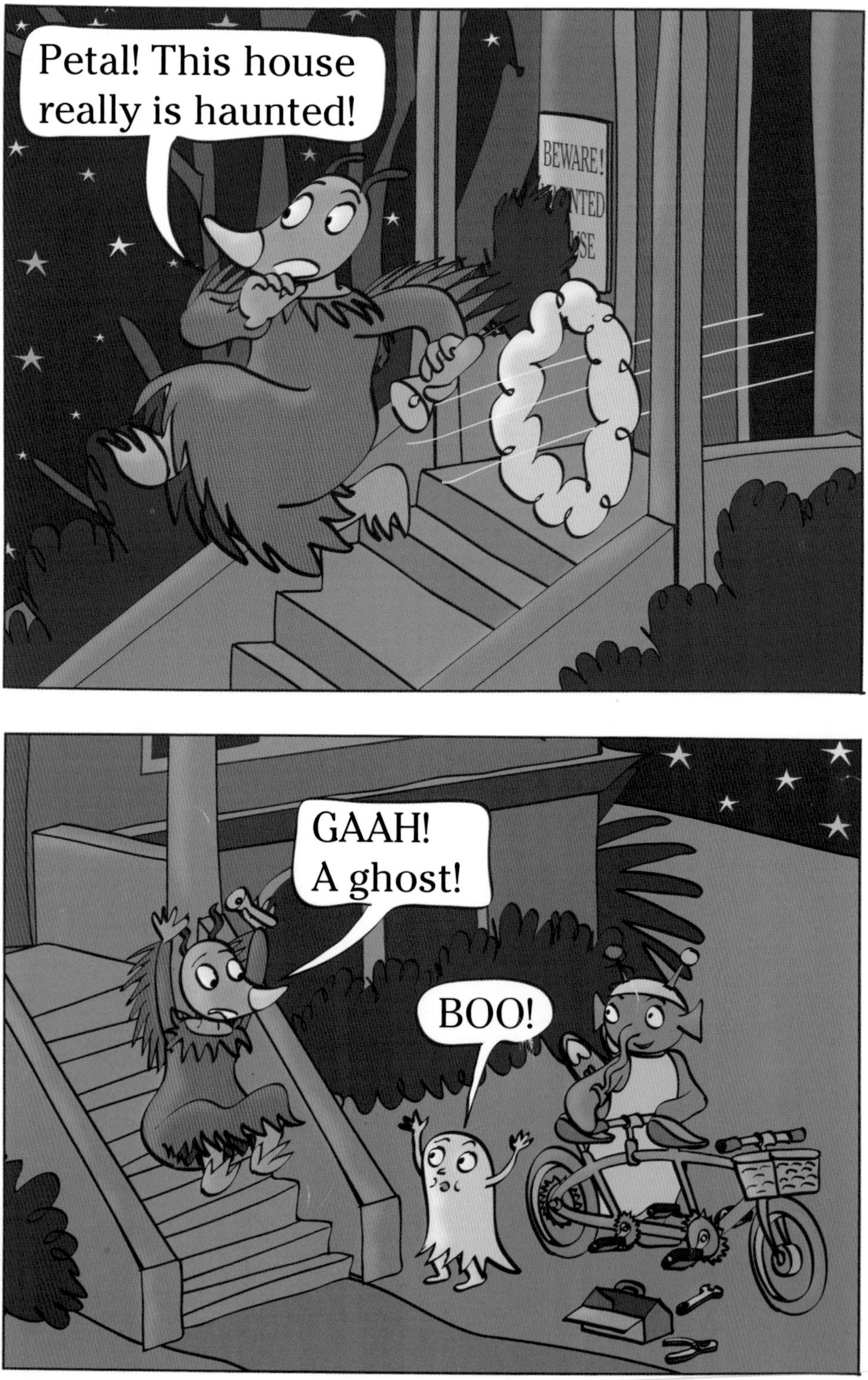
Petal! This house really is haunted!
BEWARE!
GAAH! A ghost!
BOO!

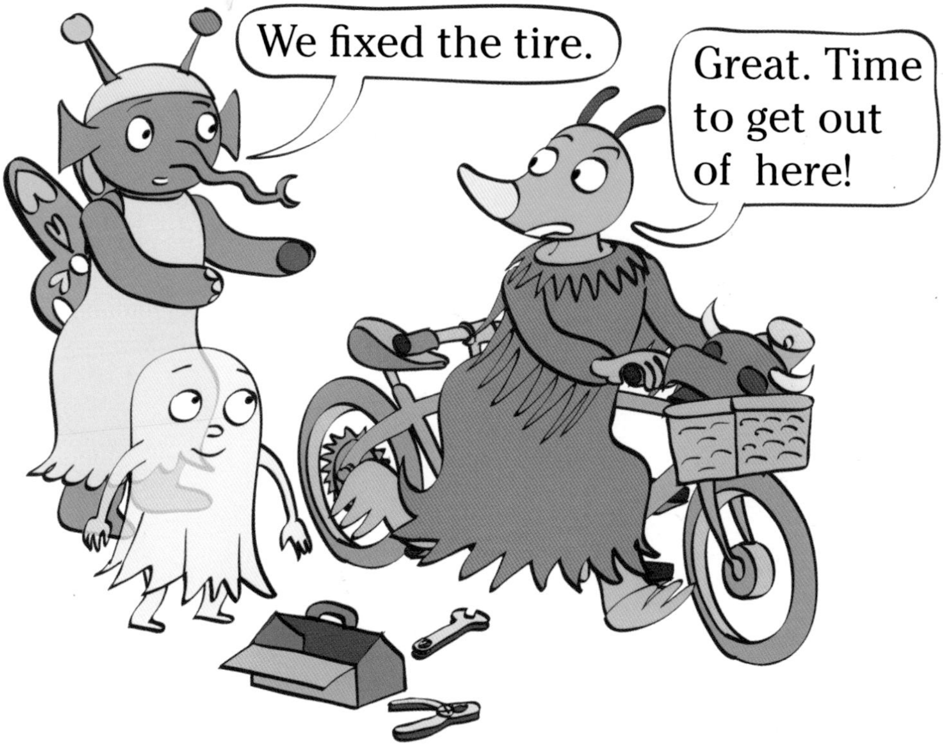
We fixed the tire.
Great. Time to get out of here!

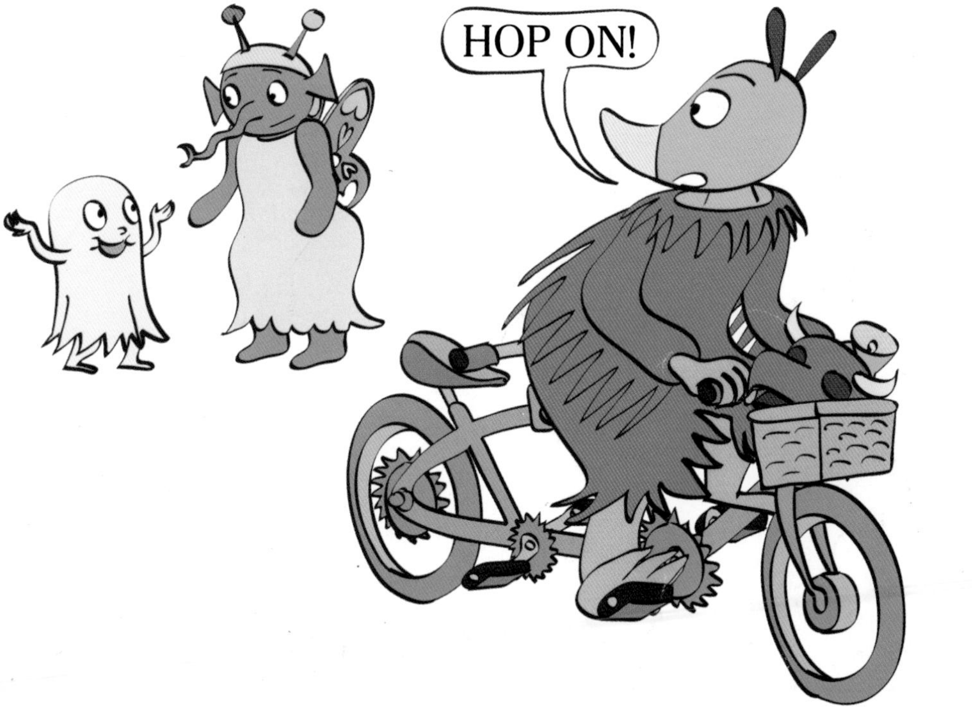
HOP ON!

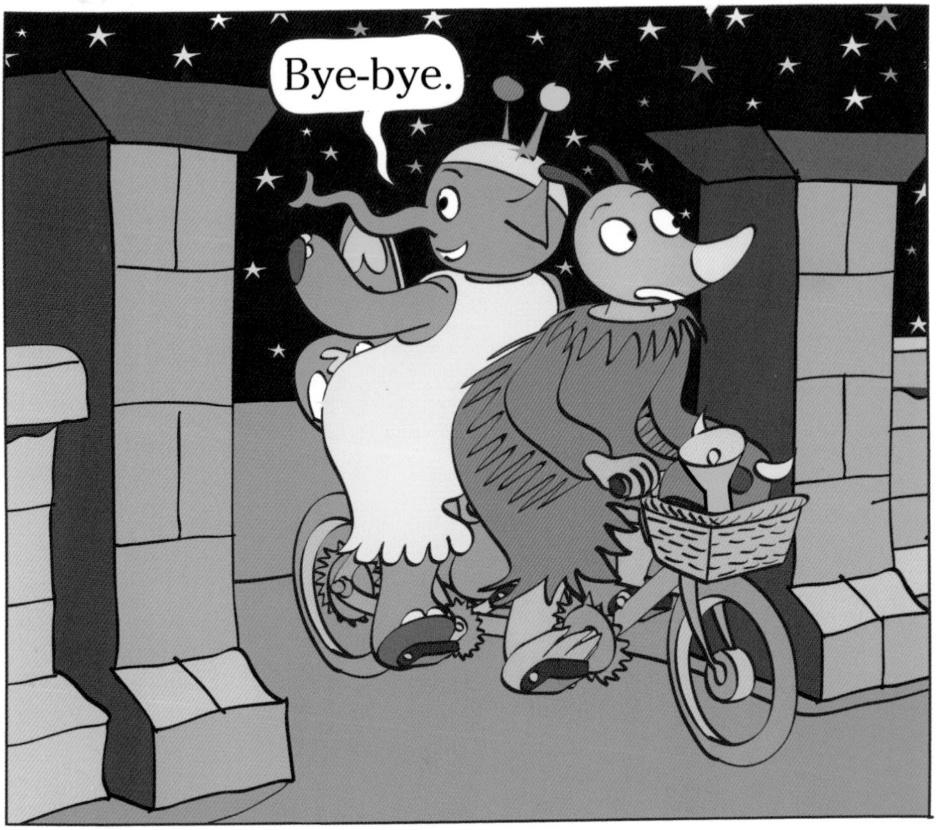
Bye-bye.

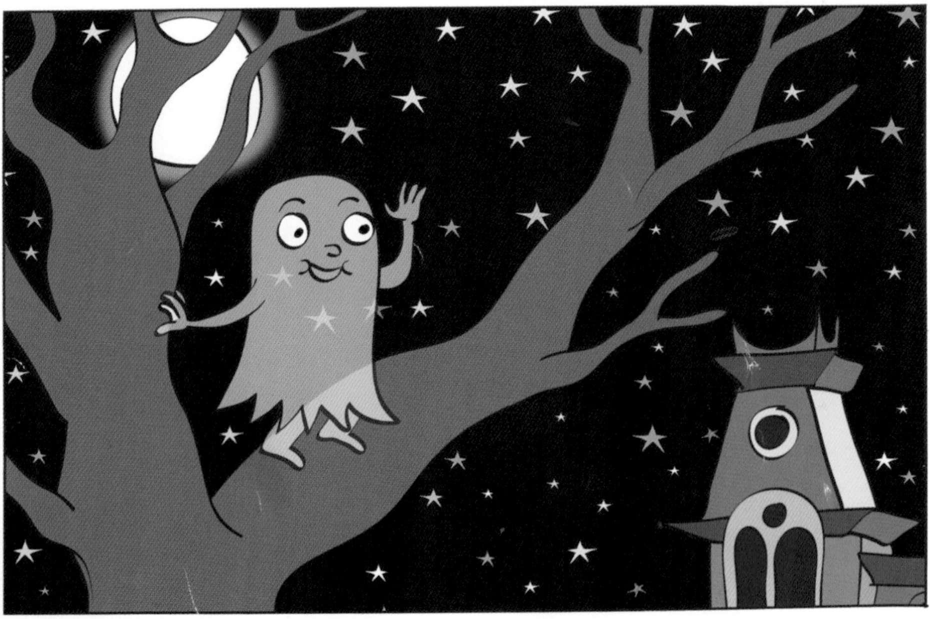

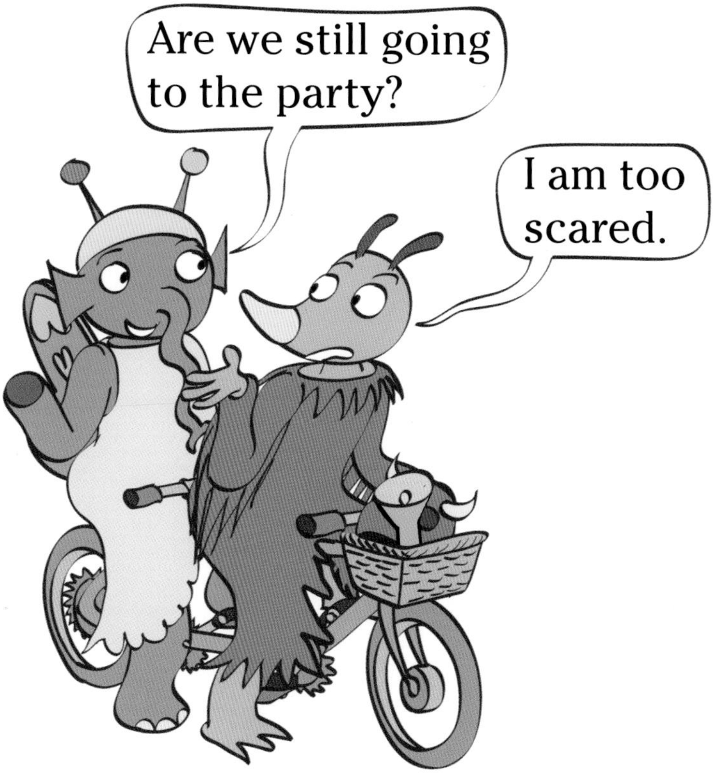
Are we still going to the party?
I am too scared.

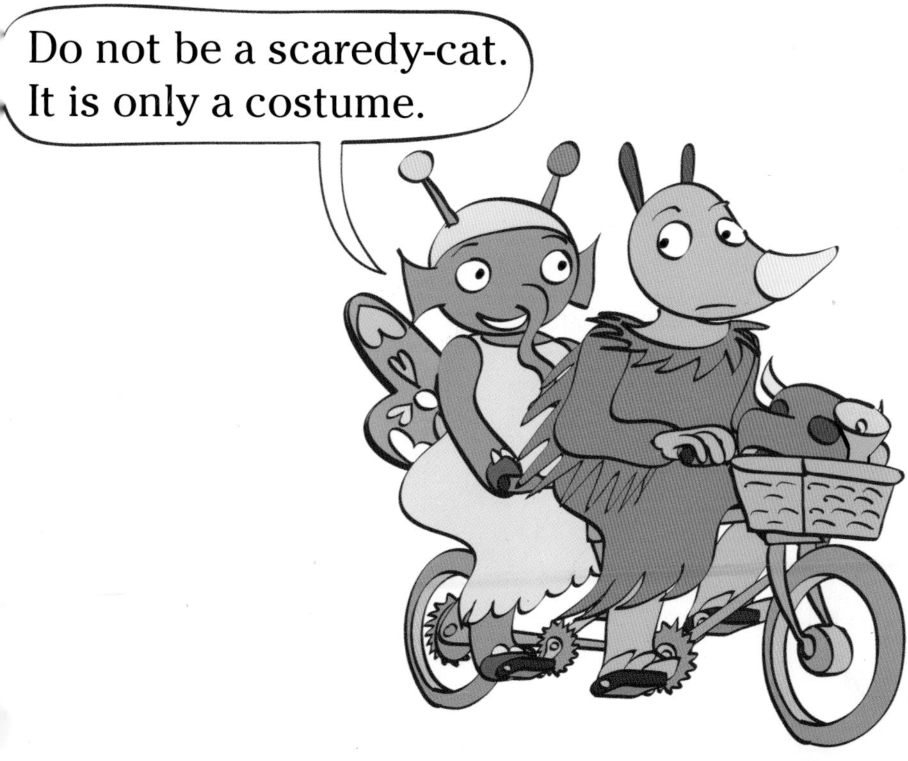
Do not be a scaredy-cat. It is only a costume.

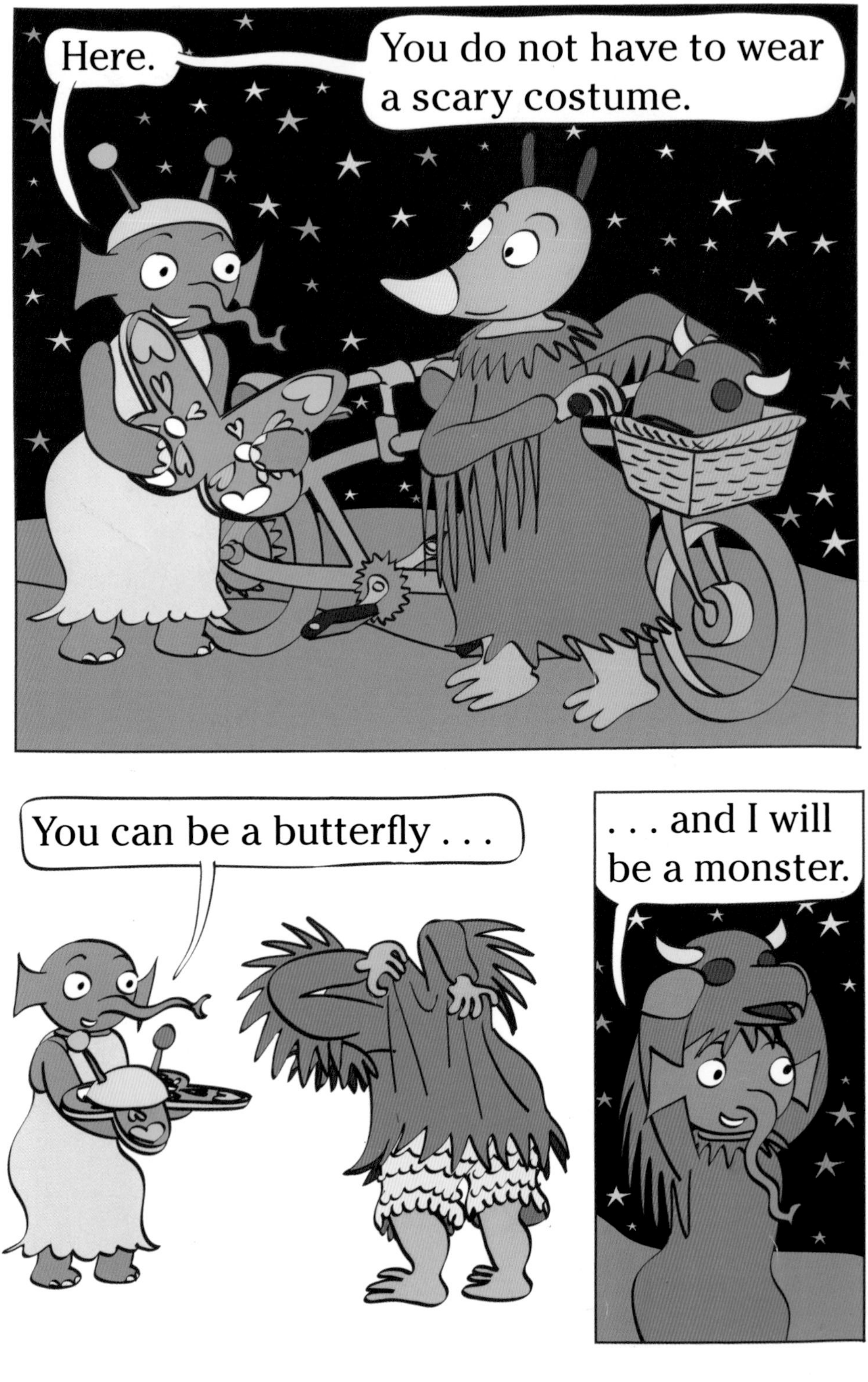
Here.
You do not have to wear a scary costume.
You can be a butterfly . . .
. . . and I will be a monster.

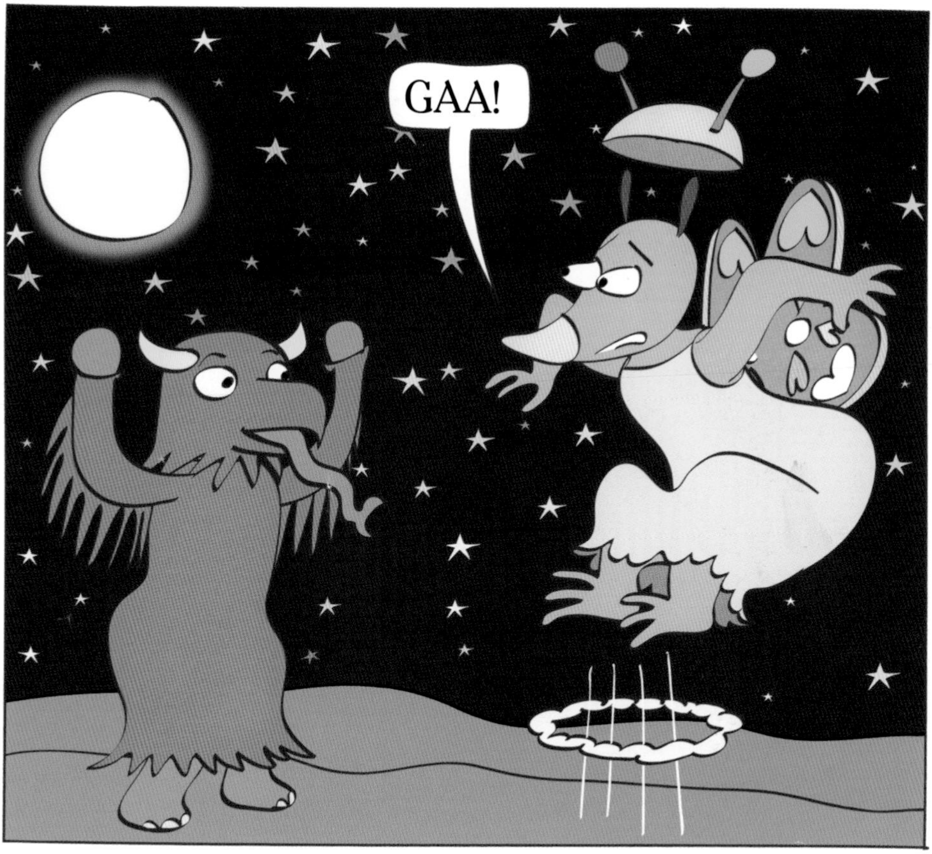
GAA!

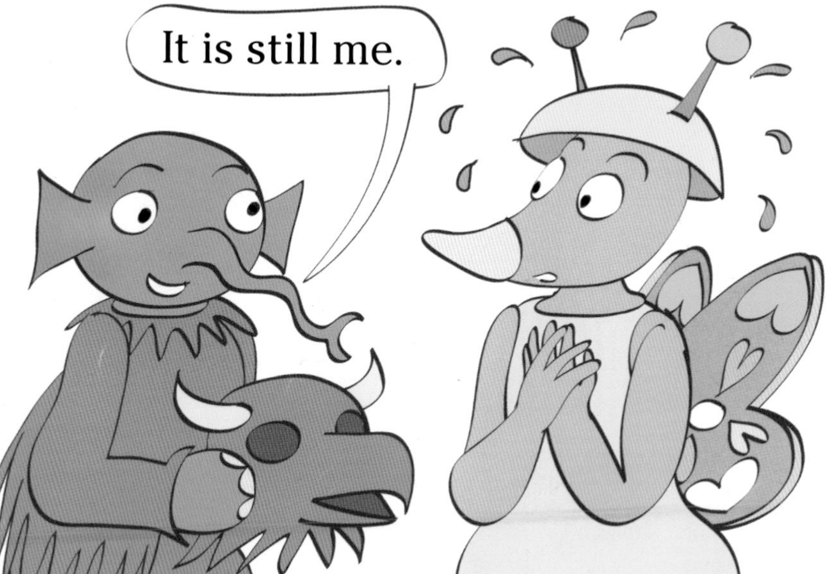
It is still me.

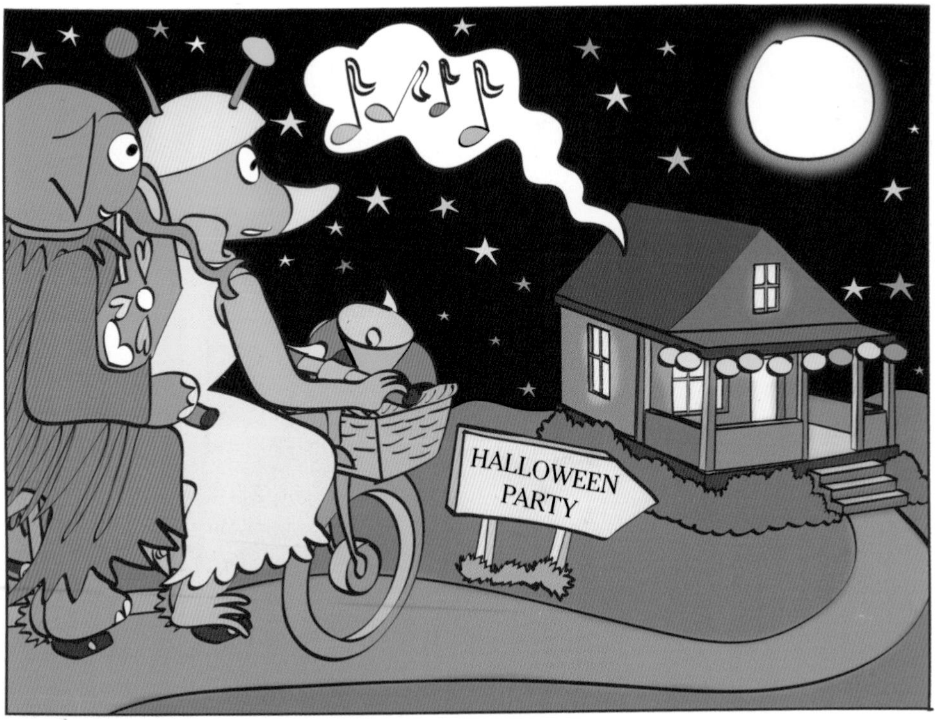
HALLOWEEN
PARTY

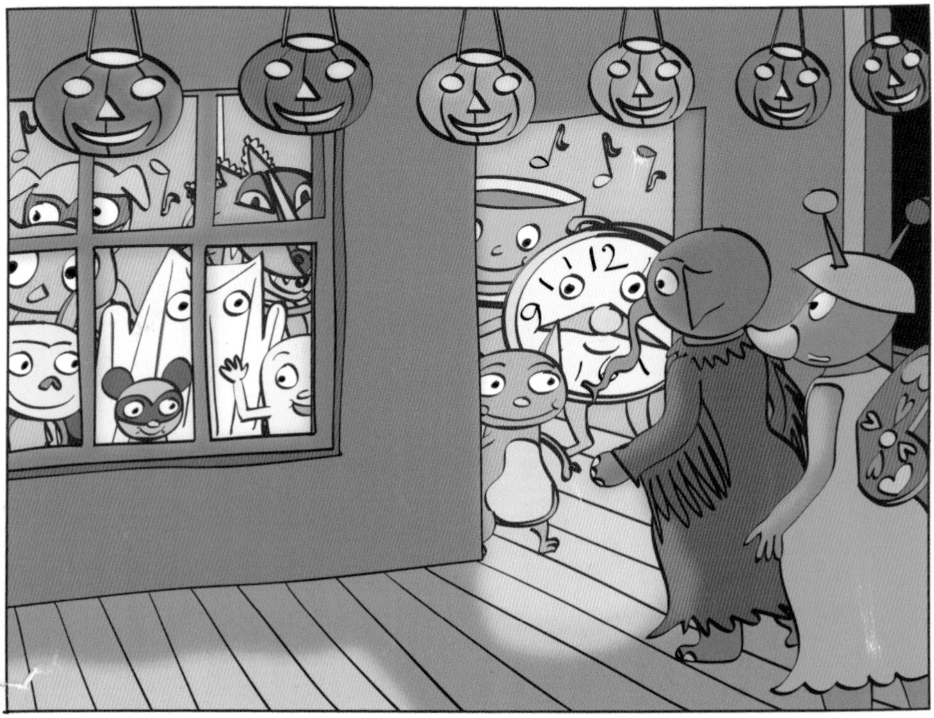

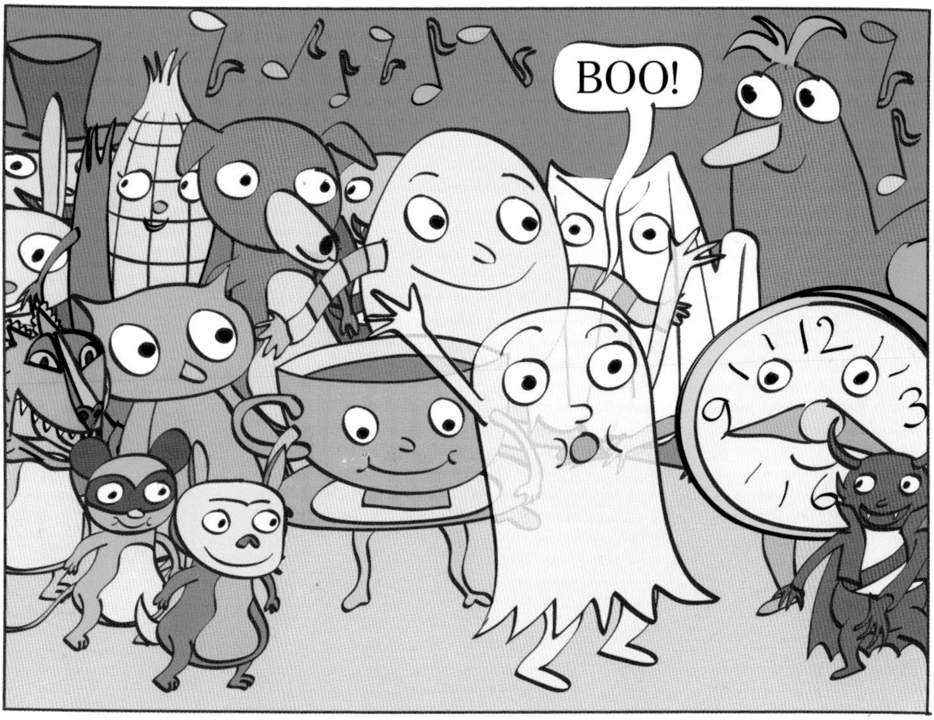
BOO!

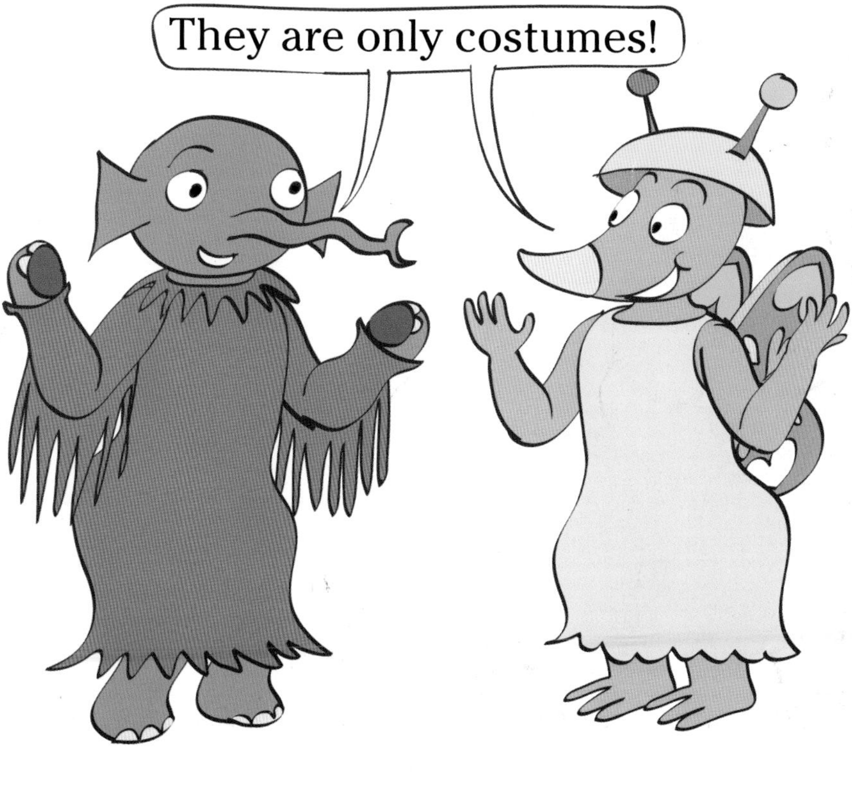
They are only costumes!

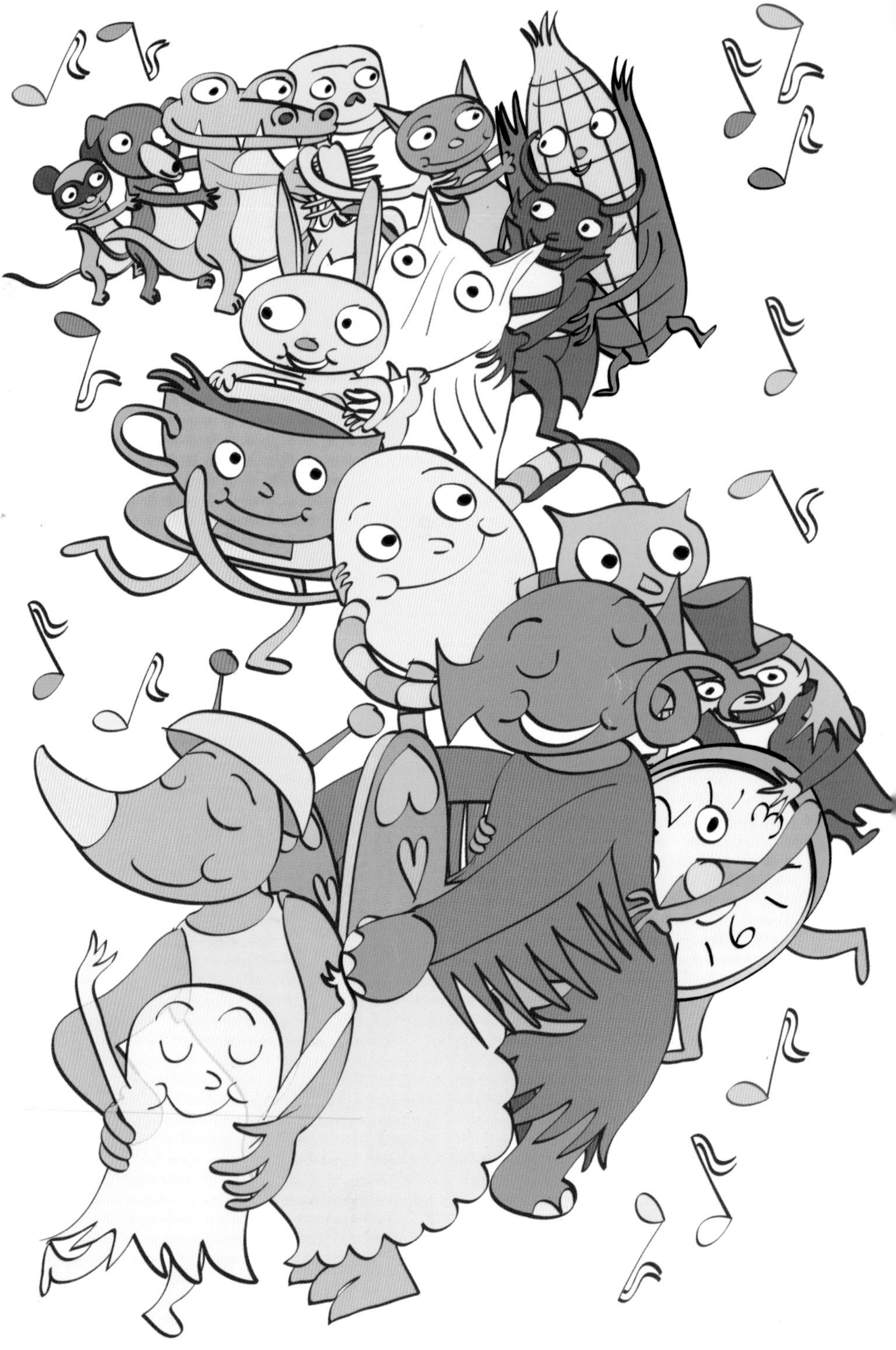